# SECRETS OF MELLIN COVE

After Wenna discovers a shocking family secret, she flies to the comfort of her beloved Cornish moors. What can she do? If she reveals the terrible truth, her family will be ruined. If she does nothing, she could be condemning the crew of a sailing ship to death. Perhaps she should confide in the tall stranger who rides past her every day, always casting an interested glance in her direction. But would he understand, or would he go straight to the authorities? No, she couldn't trust a stranger . . . or could she?

*Books by Rena George*
*in the Linford Romance Library:*

DANGER AT MELLIN COVE
ANOTHER CHANCE
TRUST IN ME
WHERE MOONBEAMS DANCE
MISTRESS OF MELLIN COVE
A MOMENT LIKE THIS

RENA GEORGE

# SECRETS OF MELLIN COVE

*Complete and Unabridged*

LINFORD
*Leicester*

First published in Great Britain in 2016

First Linford Edition
published 2017



*A catalogue record for this book is available from the British Library.*

ISBN 978–1–4448–3363–8

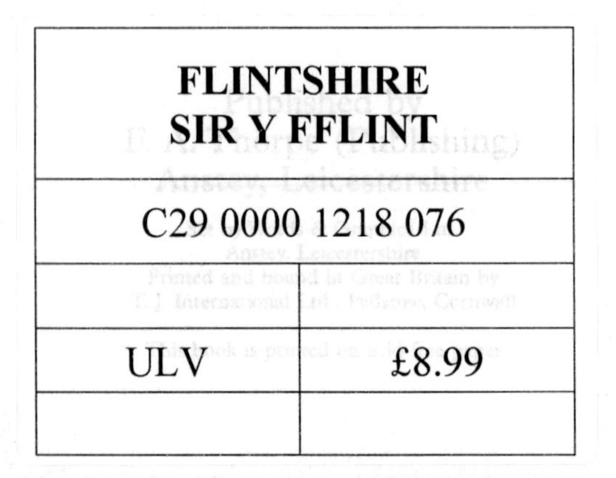

# A Smuggler's Song

If you wake at Midnight, and hear
  a horse's feet,
Don't go drawing back the blind,
  or looking in the street,
Them that ask no questions isn't
  told a lie.
Watch the wall my darling while
  the Gentlemen go by.

Five and twenty ponies,
Trotting through the dark —
Brandy for the Parson, 'Baccy for
  the Clerk.
Laces for a lady; letters for a spy.
Watch the wall my darling while
  the Gentlemen go by!

Rudyard Kipling

# 1

The wind soughed across the top of the cliffs, buffeting the coffin bearers and causing the younger ones to struggle against its force. They were taking their lead from the two men in front, their backs ramrod straight as they bore their burden along the rocky path. The women and other mourners had fallen in behind, their expressions grim as the stiff breeze smarted their eyes and tugged at the hems of their long skirts.

Out across the sea, black clouds were rolling in, heralding an oncoming storm, but no one noticed as the solemn crocodile of people made its slow progress along the winding path to the little church on the side of the hill. As the funeral party approached, groups of solemn-faced villagers parted. No one wanted to impede the progress of the coffin bearers.

All eyes were on Sally Pentreath as she pulled her black shawl closer, held her head high, and followed her husband's body into the little chapel. She could feel the tremble of her daughter-in-law Hedra's hand on her arm, and knew the young woman was also fighting back tears.

Sally gave Hedra's hand a pat and bent to whisper, 'You shouldn't be here. You should be home with your babies.'

'The babies are fine,' Hedra whispered back. 'Jane is caring for them, and I have every faith in her capability.'

Sally tried not to stare at the polished oak coffin as the two women took their places on the front pew. She didn't doubt Jane's capability, but it didn't lessen her concern for Hedra. It had been barely two weeks since she'd given birth to her twins. Sally's mouth twitched into an involuntary smile, remembering the joy in Sam's eyes as he'd gazed down at the two precious little bundles that were his new grandchildren. Her glance strayed back to the coffin and she took a shuddering breath, blinking hard for fear the tears would fall.

Hedra caught Sally's sudden emotion and offered the white lace handkerchief she was clutching, but her mother-in-law waved it away as her two elder sons, Hedra's husband Jem and his older brother Hal, took their seats alongside them.

Turning to her three younger children in the pew behind, Sally gave a reassuring smile. She nodded to Hedra's father, Matthew St Neot, as he slid in beside the young Pentreaths, and felt the pressure of his reassuring hand on her shoulder.

The Rev Collett took his place at the head of the coffin and let his solemn gaze fall on the congregation. Outside, the wind was stirring. Flurries of leaves and loose bracken gusted through the open door, where the rest of the mourners who could find no space in the chapel stood outside in respectful silence. The organ struck up and two hundred voices rose as one, their sound filling the church and echoing across the damp hillside.

The Rev. Collett waited until the last strains of the hymn had died away before raising his head. 'All of us gathered here today knew Sam Pentreath . . . knew what a good, honest, industrious man he was. His family was his life.' He broke off to smile across at Sally. 'A quiet, gentle soul who was content with life on his beloved Gribble Farm. He toiled the earth to provide for Sally and their five children, but he provided more than food. He passed his integrity on to his children and was so proud of all of them.'

He glanced at Hal and gave a kindly smile. 'Hal, the eldest, worked with his father in the fields, sowing the seed, gathering in the crops and tending to the animals on the farm.'

He nodded towards Jem. 'Everyone here knows Jem, too. Indeed, some of you have gone to sea with him on the *Sally P* and the *Bright Star*. Sam's life was in farming, but he loved the sea; and although he was not actively involved in the fishing, he was proud of the work his son provided within the community.'

The rain started ten minutes later while the Rev Collett was still eulogizing about the life of Sam Pentreath. It could be heard drumming on the grey headstones in the churchyard. Sally cast a concerned glance to the open door. She was picturing their friends huddling on the hillside, the women drawing their coarse woollen shawls closer, the men hunching against the rain. Jem followed her gaze and flicked a look back to the clergyman. The old man caught the message and brought his eulogy to an end. He signalled to the organist to strike up the closing hymn, and the strains of the music filled the church.

The earlier grief in Sally's eyes had changed to concern as she stood by her husband's open grave and peered through the rain at the others. All of them were wet through, but no one seemed to notice. Her friends were too focused on their sadness to pay any attention to their discomfort. Neither did they notice the young stranger in their midst.

Wenna had seen the crowded churchyard from her vantage point up in the field of the stone circle. She had been coming to the same spot almost every day recently. It was a place where she could daydream, where she could feel she was really herself . . . a place where she could sketch.

It was here that she had first seen him. She'd glanced up from her sketchbook that morning as the rider came into view. His horse had been limping, and the man had dismounted to lead the old mare along the rutted lane. He'd glanced into the field as he passed, but her presence behind one of the standing stones had been well hidden.

Her heart had given an unexpected flutter as she flicked over to a clean page of her sketchbook and began to draw. Her charcoal had flown across the page, outlining the well-defined face, the dark hair falling untidily to his shoulders, and his tall stature. His clothes had been those of a man who had no care for fashion, and he certainly could not have been described as handsome. But as she'd watched him lead his horse along the lane, her heart had raced. She'd had no idea who the stranger was, but the feelings that had stirred inside her had been unnerving.

She had seen him many times after that. They could have been on nodding terms if she hadn't been so shy.

Wenna's father, Sir George Quintrell, was a Member of Parliament, and much against her will he had insisted on her joining him in London for a week. She knew it was a plan concocted by her stepmother, probably with more than a little help from her grandmother. They were determined to persuade her to live up to her name, Lady Rowenna Quintrell. But Wenna had other ideas.

The London trip had, however, meant it had been some time before she'd been able to return to her stone circle.

As always, the sketchbook had been tucked under her arm as she'd walked to her field that morning. Grey clouds scudded across the sky, and the wind that danced across the moors brought the smell of rain with it. She'd changed from the blue cotton day gown her grandmother had so approved of, and into the breeches and gilet she preferred. Her pale flowing hair was pinned up into a topknot and tucked beneath her cap. Dressed like this, no one would ever suspect she was a girl, let alone Lady Rowenna, which was exactly the way Wenna wanted it.

She had slipped out unnoticed by even the servants, and run the half-mile along the road to her field. By the time she reached it, the sea was black, reflecting the angry-looking sky. Even from this distance she could hear the waves surging noisily against the rocks at the foot of the cliffs.

In the distance she could see the little church, and the churchyard black with people. She blinked. A wedding? But no. This wasn't the kind of day for a wedding. None of the people looked particularly festive. That left only one option: a funeral was taking place at Mellin Cove Church.

Wenna tucked her sketchbook inside her unfashionable waistcoat, hardly noticing the rain as she ran across the fields.

No one questioned that she was a stranger. She stood in the crowd, watching as the funeral party emerged from the church led by an elderly clergyman. The coffin bearers came next, followed by the rest of the grieving family members. As they approached, Wenna's heart missed a beat. It was *him* — the rider she'd seen pass her field.

A wave of excitement swept over her, and then a feeling of panic. She had to control the urge to flee. If she ran, and he saw her, he might demand to know what business she had here. She would be humiliated.

But she needn't have worried. The sadness in the man's eyes told her he would notice no stranger that day. As she stared at him, she realized she had been wrong to have thought him not handsome. Even now, with his face etched with grief, he held such an attraction.

He and another man who resembled him were the lead pallbearers. She tried to guess who was in the coffin. It was obviously someone he had loved. She bowed her head as they passed, not lifting it again until the coffin had been placed by the open grave. Wenna had never witnessed a funeral before; she had been only five when her dear mother passed on. A tear stung her eye. The sadness around her was a living thing, and she was getting caught up in the emotion of it. As the burial continued, she averted her eyes, not able to bear seeing the distress in the man's face.

She scanned the crowd for any sign of Annie. It looked as though the whole of Mellin Cove was in the churchyard, but no matter how hard she searched she couldn't see Annie or her husband Jory.

Wenna had been devastated when the couple had left Boscawen House. Annie had been her mother's maid. She had married Jory Rosen, Boscawen's gardener, and together they moved into the small cottage on the estate. As Wenna grew older she'd visited Annie every day, and took it as a personal insult when the couple announced they were leaving Boscawen. Annie, apparently, had always had a hankering to return to Mellin Cove, the village where she had been brought up.

Wenna missed them both desperately, but she had been too proud to admit it, and certainly not to Annie. But now that she was here, she had a sudden longing to renew that old friendship again. She took one more glance around the crowd. It was odd that Annie and Jory were not here. Whoever the deceased was, they must surely have known them?

* * *

Hedra moved closer to Sally, aware that her mother-in-law wanted to reach out to some of the older women who looked so uncomfortable under their sodden, matted shawls. Everyone stood aside as the coffin bearers, led by Jem and Hal, lowered Sam's body into the grave. Wet eyes were indistinguishable from the weather-lashed faces as the Rev Collett uttered some more words of respect for Sam. Every pair of eyes had turned to the grave — every pair except Wenna's, and one more. Enor Vingoe's gaze was fixed on Hedra's brother, Kit St Neot.

Hedra had noticed the man earlier as the family went into the church. She hadn't given him much thought at the time; but now, watching the way he stared so earnestly at her brother, she wondered what business a stranger would have at a Mellin Cove funeral.

The Pentreath family gathered around their mother. Hal, the eldest, put an arm round Sally's shoulders as she held out her arms to the two youngest children, Queenie and Kadan. Luk, who was twenty-one, stood beside his mother.

Jem came to stand with Hedra and hissed under his breath to her, 'What are they doing here?'

Hedra looked across the churchyard to where Lady Carolyn Trevanion and her father, wealthy mine owner Sir Bartholomew, stood. The glances the young woman was openly directing to Kit made her bristle. Carolyn had done her best in the past to split up Kit and Dewi. The fact that they were now happily married apparently made no difference to her. She was so obviously still intent on pursuing him.

'There's your answer,' Hedra said, inclining her head towards Kit.

Jem sighed. 'The woman is shameless

— and her father is no better. How can he show his face in Mellin Cove when he is responsible for so many deaths? Thanks to his greed and irresponsibility, there are children here who are now orphans.'

Hedra reached for Jem's hand. One of his closest friends, Roger Rowle, had died when a shaft collapsed in Wheel Maura. It was Trevanion's mine, and the blood of the dead miners was on his hands. He'd had a responsibility to keep his miners safe, but he had let them down.

Jem had been in no doubt that if the mine had been properly maintained, the accident would not have happened. And now here they were, father and daughter, still showing no signs of remorse. Jem had been about to step over to them and demand to know what they were doing at his father's funeral. They were no friends of the Pentreaths. But Hal beat him to it.

Hedra saw him square up to Trevanion and gripped Jem's arm. 'You must stop him,' she urged. 'This is not the place for confrontations.'

But it was Sally who stepped forward. 'You're not welcome in Mellin Cove,' she said. 'Please leave before there is any trouble. I will have no disrespect at my husband's funeral.'

Sir Bartholomew Trevanion tipped his hat to her, but she could see the red stain of anger flush his neck. 'That was never my intention, Mistress Pentreath,' he said stiffly. 'My daughter and I came here to pay our respects. Of course, if we are not wanted . . . '

Jem moved to stand with his mother and brother. 'You are *not* wanted here, sir. Please leave now,' he said. Out of the corner of her eye, Hedra could see Kit and her father also closing in on the Trevanions. She couldn't believe Carolyn still had the boldness to smile at her brother.

The crowd cleared a path for the pair to leave the churchyard. Hedra watched them go before turning to Dewi with a sigh. 'Can you believe the audacity of some people?'

'That woman makes me feel so uneasy,' Dewi said. 'It's as though I didn't exist; as though Kit and I were not married. Carolyn still flutters her eyelashes at him. I try not to get annoyed, but it so infuriates me.'

Hedra smiled. 'Don't let Carolyn get under your skin. That's what she wants. It's a game to her.'

'It's a game I'm not playing,' Dewi said. 'And neither is Kit.'

# 2

Annie was stirring a pot of simmering broth when Jory strolled into the kitchen. 'They'll be more'n a few that thanks you for that when the boats come back,' he said, wrapping his great arms around his wife's waist and giving her a squeeze.

'Be off with you, man,' she laughed, struggling free, 'or you'll get this spoon over your head.'

Jory sniffed at the appetizing vegetables over her shoulder. It had been almost a year since they opened the kiddley in the disused fish store at the far end of Mellin Cove harbour. It had been Annie's idea, and as far as he was concerned, the best one she'd ever had.

Annie often thought that fate must have played a hand on the day she came back to the cove. Her parents, Amy and Nathaniel Vingoe, were long gone, but the cottage where she grew up was still standing, if a little rundown. She and Jory had wandered around it, rubbing the grime from the windows to squint inside. Nostalgia had engulfed her with no warning and she'd found herself with tears trickling down her cheeks.

'You want to come back here, don't you?' Jory had said quietly from behind her. Annie had thought of their modest cottage in the grounds of Boscawen House. She remembered how Jory came through the door each night and sank exhausted onto one of the spindly homemade chairs, his face and hands thick with the grime of the gardens.

'How do you feel about moving to Mellin Cove, my love?' she'd asked, still trying to peer through the cottage windows.

'I'm no fisherman,' Jory had said, 'and from what I saw up on the moors there, the only mine chimney I could spy was a distance away.'

Annie had turned, her eyes shining. 'I'm not asking you to be a miner, or even a gardener again. What if we had a new way of earning a crust?'

Jory had frowned. 'There is no other way. What are you talking about, woman?'

'This!' Annie had said, opening her arms to the cottage. She'd turned to the nearly derelict old building beside it. 'And this!'

They had climbed the winding path to Mellin Hall together. Annie had never met Kit St Neot. In her day it had been the Constantine family who owned the Mellin Cove estate, including the cottages clustered around the old harbour. As a girl she had worked briefly at the Hall as a very lowly kitchen maid. That was in the days of Sir Edward Constantine. She fought back the anger that rose inside her at the very thought of his name. Her sister Mary had died because of that man. Until then, she had considered him a kindly soul; but she had been wrong.

What happened to Mary had been especially difficult for her to deal with because the Constantines had been good to her family — good to every family in Mellin Cove. But she couldn't change the past. Even though the man was long dead, she would never forgive him.

Kit St Neot had inherited Mellin Hall and the estate through a family connection — an Uncle Thomas who had married Edward's daughter, Morwenna. Kit himself was a complete stranger to her. Would he consider her an upstart for asking to rent the old place, especially when she explained her plan? She'd heard stories about the man's wicked uncle, Edgar St Neot, and an evil band of smugglers and wreckers he'd been associated with. He'd been all for raising the tenants' rents, while at the same time allowing the Hall and estate to fall into decline.

She had also heard of the man's fury when his brother's will was read and he hadn't inherited Mellin Hall and the cove as he'd expected. It had gone to his young nephew, Kit. In retribution,

Edgar had tried to destroy the fishing fleet, but had died in the very fire that he'd caused.

Annie remembered how nervous she'd been that day when she stood at the kitchen door of Mellin Hall asking to see Mr St Neot. Tomas Sweet, one of the few original servants still at the Hall, had been kind to them and had shown her and Jory into the grand front room to wait. She smiled now at the memory of how Kit's eyebrow had arched in surprise when she put her idea to him. He could have ordered them out, there and then, but he hadn't. He had listened carefully to everything Annie had said.

'The cottage you mention is not occupied at present, and it does need more than a bit of work to get it habitable again,' he had said.

'That will not be a problem, sir.' Annie had looked from Kit to Jory. 'We could soon knock the old place into shape.'

'Then I am happy to offer you the

tenancy.' Kit stroked his chin. 'As for your other suggestion . . . I'm not sure I could sanction an unlicensed kiddley-wink in Mellin Cove.'

'We would be more interested in providing good wholesome meals for hungry fishermen and travellers than simply just selling ale to them,' she emphasized. 'We could also build up a stock of provisions — vegetables, milk and the like from local farms — to sell.'

Jory touched her arm to warn her she was becoming too enthusiastic. She saw Kit pursing his lips as he'd considered the idea.

'I can see the merits of your proposal, but let me think about it. In the meantime, I see no reason why you should not move into the cottage at your convenience.'

Annie had to stop herself from throwing her arms around the man's neck.

She and Jory had moved into the cottage the very next week. A month after that, Kit St Neot had appeared at their door. He had given Annie's proposal some more thought. He could see they were good and responsible tenants, and so, provided they concentrated more on selling food and provisions than ale, he would be happy to go along with the plan for a kiddley.

In fact he did more. The very next day, Kit and Tomas turned up to help her and Jory to restore the old fish store to a workable space. And now she stretched her back and looked around her. They had turned the once disused structure into a prosperous business, and the cottage next door into a cosy home.

'We are so lucky, Jory,' she told him for the umpteenth time.

'And it will stay that way as long as the village menfolk enjoy their ale and have a taste for your broth.'

Annie nodded. The only black cloud on their horizon was Enor Vingoe, Annie's great nephew. As a special favour to his parents, Peder and his wife Rebecca, they had agreed to Enor living with them until the summer in exchange for his help serving in the kiddley bar.

Annie had a special fondness for Peder, as he was the illegitimate son of her late sister, Mary. She could hardly have refused Mary's grandson a place under their roof.

So they had kept their side of the bargain; but after an initial few hours serving ale to thirsty fishermen, Enor always managed to find an excuse to wander off. And now Annie was seriously regretting her rash decision to allow him to stay.

* * *

Wenna hadn't seen him at first, so his presence in the churchyard took her by surprise. Withdrawing behind a moss-covered headstone, Wenna watched Hal as he knelt by the freshly dug grave and laid his hand on the moist earth. His lips were moving, but she was too far away to hear his words.

Although she had been in the crowd of mourners at the funeral, she hadn't been able to establish who had actually died. Was the man's wife buried here? She had ruled out that it was a child because of the size and apparent weight of the coffin. A shiver ran through Wenna. She was torn between feelings of guilt for even witnessing such a private moment, and compassion for the man's sadness. She longed to go to him, touch his shoulder, tell him she understood. But she couldn't reveal her presence.

Hal thought he'd caught a glimpse of movement out of the comer of his eye as he got to his feet. He scanned the churchyard, but all was still. He waited, listening, wheeling round when he heard the footfall behind him, and broke into a smile when he recognized the short, stocky figure of the Rev William Collett. The man spoke with a distinct wheeze.

'Ah, Hal. I'm glad that I caught you. I was sure it was you; I saw you from my study window. I don't mean to intrude, but I just wondered how your dear mother is bearing up.'

'It's early days, Reverend.' Hal sighed. 'As you know, Pa had not been a well man for many a year, but none of us expected him to go like that.' He raised his eyes, staring out across the sea. 'He was ploughing that north field with me only four days ago.'

The Rev Collett gave a sad nod. 'The Lord works in mysterious ways, my boy. At least Sam did not suffer, so we must be glad for small mercies.'

Hal couldn't see that his father's death was any kind of mercy; not when it caused his mother so much distress and mapped out his own future in a way he would now have to accept. A year ago he would have relished the responsibility of taking over the farm, but that was before he'd got a taste for the sea. Farming was no longer in his blood, if it ever had been. He'd never been given a choice: as the eldest of the five Pentreath children, it was expected of him that he would follow in his father's footsteps and run Gribble Farm.

The restlessness had only begun to settle in this past year as he watched his younger brother Jem grow his fleet of fishing boats. There were two of them at the moment, the *Sally P* — named after their mother — and the *Bright Star*. A third lugger was being built by Kit St Neot, Jem's brother-in-law, at his yard down at Dizzard Cove. The sea had always been in Jem's blood, but it had taken Hal a long time — and many invigorating fishing trips where he acted as a crewman on one or other of his brother's boats — to realize that his future could also be at sea.

'I suppose the running of Gribble Farm will now become your responsibility,' the reverend wheezed.

Hal had to force his mind back to the present. He nodded. It looked like the old man was right.

'I was thinking of calling on your mother to offer her whatever support or otherwise that she might need. Do you think she would welcome that, Hal?'

A visit from the old clergyman, no matter how well-intentioned, reminding her of what she had lost in his father's passing, was probably the last thing his ma needed right now. But she would never turn the man away. He meant well and would receive a welcome in the big farmhouse kitchen.

'I'm sure my mother would appreciate a visit.' He tried to smile but couldn't, so he just nodded.

'Don't forget to tell her I was enquiring after her,' the Rev Collett called after him, his words snatched away by the wind as Hal left the churchyard and turned up the cliff path for home.

Wenna didn't emerge from her hiding place until both men had left the churchyard. The vicar had disappeared into his house next to the church, but she could still see Hal on the cliff path, his tall frame bent against the wind. Her musings that he was visiting the grave of his wife had been wrong; Wenna had heard enough of the conversation to know that. Her heart had lurched a little when she realized it. Had that been wrong of her? It still didn't mean the man was unmarried.

She longed to approach him; ask if she could sketch him perhaps. But she knew she never would. That would hardly be the behaviour of a well-brought-up young lady. She glanced down at her muddy breeches. Not that she exactly looked like a well-brought-up lady, not dressed as she was, and with her long fair hair tied up in a topknot and wedged into her cap.

'What are you doing there, boy? State your business.'

A girl was coming towards her. Wenna jumped at the sharp tone, glancing around to see who she could be addressing, and then realized it was her. The girl had thought she was a boy. She looked down again at her dark breeches and brown leather gilet. It wasn't difficult to understand her mistake.

'Did you hear me, boy?' The girl was advancing towards her. 'What are you doing here?'

This was no time to take offence. Her current appearance could work in her favour. Wenna pulled the skip of her cap over her face and kept her eyes on the ground.

'I 'ave business with the reverend,' she mumbled, trying to keep her voice as low and gruff as possible.

'What business?' the girl asked sharply.

'It's private. Will ee fetch 'im or not?' She could feel the girl's curious eyes on her. At first she thought she would refuse and tell her to be on her way, but she didn't.

'Wait here. I'll ask my father if he will see you.' Her skirts rustled as she turned and marched back to the house.

It was the chance Wenna needed to make her escape.

# 3

Hedra had been looking out to sea when she spotted Hal on the cliff path. As he passed the cottage, her first instinct was to call out to him; but something about the dogged slope of his shoulders, his head bowed into the wind, suggested he wanted to be alone. She sighed and went back to her seat by the fire.

'Poor Hal,' she said. 'He's taking this badly.'

'We are all taking it badly,' Jem said, his eyes on the leaping flames.

'I know that, my love, but Hal seemed especially close to Sam. What I mean is . . . well, you have been away at sea so much that you've not spent as much time with your father as perhaps the others have.'

'I loved my father,' Jem said quietly.

Hedra got up and ran across the

room, gathering him into her arms. 'Of course you did, my darling. I was not suggesting otherwise, and if it sounded like that then I apologize. I only meant — '

Jem pulled her onto his knee. 'I know what you meant. My life is taken up with the boats.'

'You're at sea half of the week.'

'Tending the land was never for me. Father knew that; and besides, there was Hal doing such a good job. They didn't need me.'

Jem was speaking thoughtfully, for although he seldom admitted it to himself, he felt guilty. No one ever questioned how hard and dangerous it was to make a living from fishing, but it was a life he enjoyed. Even now he could feel the wind on his face and the muscles in his back rippling as he hauled the nets back on board. Sometimes there would be a mass of squirming silver fish in them, but there were plenty of other times when the sea was not so generous. He sighed. It was a living — and sometimes there was more. He was remembering those trips to France and the cargoes they collected that provided enough bounty to feed the entire village.

Everyone, except the excise men, turned a blind eye to the smuggling. Jem knew it was illegal — all of them did — but the truth was that Mellin Cove would not survive without it. Every man, woman and child turned out to help haul the chests of tea and kegs of brandy ashore. They were stored in a cave in the hill behind the cottages until they could be collected by the agent and the proceeds divided out. It was dangerous, though. All it would take would be one loose tongue and the revenue men would be on them, searching every inch of beach and hillside. Every cottage would be invaded, and soldiers had no respect for the homes of fisher folk. Jem and the others risked losing their boats — but all of them could lose their lives. Ways could be found to make smuggling a hanging offence.

He sighed. They must all be extra-cautious now. Mellin Cove could not afford to be exposed. His father was well aware of all this, and had never criticized him. Sam had been as proud of his fisherman son as he'd been of the rest of his family.

Jem was thinking about Hal — tall, wide-chested and strong. In his mind's eye he could see his brother's long stride as he crossed the rutted field pushing a wheelbarrow laden with tates. He smiled at the thought of his two younger brothers on their knees harvesting the crops, and his sister standing by the kitchen door, laughing. Their mother Sally would be in the kitchen baking bread, rolling up her sleeves with floury hands and lifting the heavy tray to carry it across to the oven.

When Jem decided to become a fisherman, life at Gribble Farm had carried on without him. He suddenly felt incredibly sad.

'I did wonder if Hal would leave the

farm and join you at the fishing full-time,' Hedra said. 'From what he told me, he certainly seemed to enjoy it.'

Jem gave another sigh. It was true, Hal did love going to sea with him. Their father had encouraged it; but then none of them had had any idea that his life was to end so unexpectedly.

Everyone knew that Sam Pentreath had been ailing for many months — well, years, if Jem were honest with himself. They were aware that he wasn't as fit as he had been in his younger days. But that was just a part of how Sam was latterly. No one had expected him to die.

Jem wished, not for the first time, that he had been there with him in the kitchen that morning. He'd heard the story secondhand from his younger brother, Luk. Sam had clutched his chest, doubled over and collapsed on the floor. That had been it. No warning. At least if he or Hal had been there, it might have made things easier for their mother. As it was, she'd had to deal with the terrible situation all on her own. He'd said as much to Hedra, and she had told him that perhaps it was the way his parents would have wanted . . . those last moments together. But Jem wasn't so sure.

'What will happen to the farm now?' Hedra asked. She had wriggled free from his knee and gone to the table to clear the tea things away onto a tray. The children were having their nap — all four of them. It was a blissful few moments that rarely happened these days in the Pentreath household.

'How do you mean, what will happen to the farm?' Jem queried.

'Well, I don't imagine that Hal is very keen to take it on again, not after what you said about him being a natural fisherman.' She paused, thinking. 'The boys are too young to run the place on their own, so I suppose Hal has no choice. His days as a fisherman are over.'

There was a knock on the door, and

Jane, the girl from the village who helped Hedra, came into the room. 'The children are all still sleeping,' she said in her gentle Cornish accent, 'but I don't expect peace will be reigning for much longer.' She glanced to the table. 'Can I take the tea things?'

'Thank you, Jane.' Hedra smiled. 'I'll go up in a minute to check on them.'

* * *

Wenna noticed the glitter of excitement in her grandmother's eyes before the guests had even arrived. She had tried to work out how a boring old ship-owner and his wife, Richard and Sarah Luscombe, could possibly make interesting dinner guests. And then she remembered that her father had been friends with the man going back many years. It still didn't explain, however, what her grandmother's interest was.

The conversation around the dinner table was as boring as Wenna had feared. How could anyone sustain interest in the weather, the latest fashions in Plymouth, and what went on in the halls of Parliament? To be fair, Mrs Luscombe had tried several times to draw her into the conversation. Wenna had replied politely, but she knew she was hardly being engaging, and eventually the woman gave up, preferring to concentrate her attention on her husband.

Wenna wondered what her mother would have made of the evening. Several times she had glanced to her stepmother, who also seemed to be focusing on Mr Luscombe. Her grandmother was nodding and smiling, with frequent inclines of her head to encourage Mrs Luscombe to say more. Wenna wondered if any of them would even remember later what any of them had spoken about around the dinner table.

She was glad when her grandmother signalled it was time for them to leave the gentlemen to their brandy while the ladies retired to the drawing room to take tea. Lady Catherine's deep-blue satin gown rustled richly as she settled herself in a chair and beckoned Wenna's stepmother and Mrs Luscombe to follow suit.

With a disguised sigh, Wenna took a seat on the chaise longue and returned Mrs Luscombe's kind smile. She was warming to the woman. Somewhere under that charming expression, she suspected the lady recognized how bored Wenna was with the proceedings. Perhaps she felt the same way. Did she have an ally here? If that were the case, then she would acknowledge that her father's guest had more intelligence than she'd originally credited her with.

One of the younger maids brought in a heavy silver tray with the tea things arranged on it, and placed it on the table in front of her grandmother. Lady Catherine flapped her hand at the girl, dismissing her. Wenna tried to catch her eye and smile, but the little maid was too busy scurrying from the room.

'It's Earl Grey,' her grandmother was

saying. 'I presume that's agreeable to you, Mrs Luscombe?'

If it wasn't, Mrs Luscombe was being given no chance to say, for her grandmother was already pouring. 'How do you take it?' She inclined her head towards their guest.

Mrs Luscombe managed a gracious smile, and Wenna wondered if she was thinking what a rude woman her grandmother was. 'Just as it comes will be fine, thank you,' she murmured.

Lady Catherine nodded, pouring the Earl Grey and handing a tea bowl across to their guest. 'I see you agree with me that any additions to a delicate brew undermines the fine flavour.'

Wenna watched the three women delicately sip from their fine china bowls and wondered what thoughts went through their heads. Twice she thought she'd caught a brief glance pass between her grandmother and step-mother. It intrigued her, and she wondered if they were signalling to each other about when to bring the silly ritual to an end. She was still contemplating this when she looked across to her grandmother and caught that unnerving glitter again.

'The high seas are such a dangerous place these days, don't you agree, Mrs Luscombe?' she said.

The woman looked up, caught off guard by the unexpected remark, and then leaned forward, placing her tea bowl and saucer carefully on the table. 'It's a constant concern for my husband. I'm sure you can understand. No vessel is truly safe when there are so many pirates in the Channel now.'

Wenna's stepmother raised an eyebrow. 'But surely cargo ships such as your husband's are no prizes for these people. I would have thought they would be after bigger fish, so to speak.' She gave a little giggle at her poor attempt at a joke, as though pleased with her wit.

Her grandmother tut-tutted. 'How do you know what cargo Mr Luscombe's ships carry, Margaret? They could be laden with gold, for all we know.'

A slight flush crept into Mrs Luscombe's cheeks and she glanced away.

'There now, you've embarrassed the poor lady. Pay no attention to my son's wife. I am sure she did not mean to be offensive.'

Margaret looked annoyed. 'Of course I didn't. I was merely suggesting that Mr Luscombe's ships may not be in such immediate danger as others.'

'But they are.' Mrs Luscombe bit her lip.

They all stared at her.

'The cargo the *Southern Star* is at this very moment on her way to collect from France is extremely valuable.'

The look that passed between Wenna's grandmother and stepmother was unmistakable this time. The idea had excited them.

'Valuable, you say?' Lady Catherine put her tea bowl and saucer back on the table.

Sarah Luscombe nodded. 'The political situation in France grows more troublesome with each passing day. The only way that noblemen across the Channel have of keeping their fortunes safe is to ship them out.'

The glitter had not left her grandmother's black eyes. 'And your husband's ship will be carrying such a cargo?'

Mrs Luscombe nodded. 'All this is in the strictest confidence, of course.'

Lady Catherine assured her their conversation would never leave the room.

Mrs Luscombe hesitated before continuing, her tone low and confiding. 'It's not the first time Richard has helped out a few of his friends in France. But each new voyage brings more fears. I've tried to persuade him to stop, but he has his loyalties.' She glanced away. 'And if truth be told, the rewards are great, and the business needs the extra income.'

Wenna could see her stepmother was

warming to this exchange. She said, 'But surely none of these pirates would know what the cargo is. How could they?'

All eyes were on Sarah Luscombe. Her narrow shoulders rose in a slow shrug. 'Who knows how people like this come by their information? I only know that they do, for many ships fall victim to their wicked attacks.'

'You really mustn't worry, my dear. I'm sure everything will be fine. I've heard tell that Cherbourg is a very safe little port where people know the value of security.'

'But the *Southern Star* sails to Roscoff, and I have it on good authority that many ships out of this port are the subject of attack.'

'Is it a really valuable cargo that your husband's ship is bringing back?' Wenna asked.

Mrs Luscombe nodded. 'Gold worth thousands of pounds — more value than the ship itself.' She lifted her eyes and stared at the far end of the room for a few moments, as though trying to collect her thoughts. And then she said, 'The ship is loaded during the night, when the harbour is in complete darkness. And then it steals out of harbour in the early hours of morning. At least, that's the plan.'

'But nothing bad has ever happened to any of your husband's ships before,' Wenna reasoned.

Sarah smiled and reached out to touch her hand. 'You're right. I'm being foolish. All will be well. I know it will.' But the shadow of doubt in the woman's eyes belied her words.

It was her father's voice Wenna could hear as the two men approached from the dining room. Mrs Luscombe's hand shot out to silence any further conversation. 'We shouldn't continue discussing this in front of my husband.' Her voice was pleading.

Lady Catherine's head nodded reassuringly. 'Women's talk, my dear. We need not bother the men with it.' Sarah flashed a grateful smile and lowered her eyes.

Wenna wondered if Mrs Luscombe was already regretting that she had been so candid about her husband's shipping activities.

# 4

Wenna did not know what had taken her to the churchyard in Mellin Cove the previous morning. Apart from at the funeral, she hadn't seen the man for more than a week. Anyway why should she be bothered? He meant nothing to her. They were complete strangers . . . And yet over the weeks he had so often looked in her direction as he rode past.

On one occasion she'd thought he would draw his horse to a halt and call over the low wall to her. He hadn't, but she could see him watching her. Was it so unusual to see a young woman sketching in a field? Such an impressive ring of standing stones would surely be an attraction for any artist. She did concede, though, that it wasn't necessary to come so far from home to sketch, not when there were plenty of lovely views from the windows of Boscawen House. If she wanted to go further afield, she could stroll down by the harbour when she had a mind to, although her grandmother would certainly not approve of that.

Boscawen Harbour was a busy, bustling kind of place where tall-masted ships came and went and merchants from nearby St Ives brought and collected their goods on horse-drawn wagons that rumbled noisily over the cobbles. The place thronged with rough seamen, bawdy language, grime and stench — and yet it fascinated Wenna. Perhaps her grandmother was right to be cautious.

Wenna entered the garden by a back gate and made for her tree. She pulled herself high up into the branches and settled into her favourite spot. It was where she did her thinking. From here she had an uninterrupted view of the lawn, all the way down to the house. She could see the mullioned windows of the drawing room, and thought she'd caught a sudden movement behind the glass. She was being watched. Someone was spying on her from behind the heavy crimson drapes. She thought of waving, but that could be construed as insolent, especially if the watcher was her grandmother. Instead she lay back against the branches, enjoying the last dappled rays of spring sunshine as she thought about Hal Pentreath.

Back at the house, Lady Catherine was shaking her head in despair at the girl in the tree. Despite her efforts, she had never managed to make a lady of Rowenna. She was a wild child with no more thought of gentility than the ruffians in the street. But as long as she was at the bottom of the garden she wouldn't disturb her, which was good as her visitors were due at any moment. She'd told them which door to approach so they wouldn't be seen — and it was well out of sight of the tree where her granddaughter was currently hiding.

* * *

Wenna woke with a start, reaching for a branch of the old oak tree to steady herself. She flexed a cramped muscle and frowned. It was never a good idea to fall asleep in a tree. The sun had sunk low in the skies and a chill wind was sweeping across the lawn, scattering the remnants of May blossom. Within the confines of her tree, she stretched and was about to climb down when a movement at the back of the house caught her eye. The early-evening gloom was settling around her, but she could still make out the two figures moving around the house.

Her first thought was that they were up to no good. They weren't the first unsavoury-looking people to visit Boscawen House. She should be used to her grandmother's questionable associates — but seeing these two skulking around the house made her insides contract. Maybe they weren't friends of her grandmother's after all. What if they were here to harm her? She watched the two figures until they disappeared around the side of the house before scrambling out of her tree to run across the grass, ever fearful that the men would reappear. But they didn't.

She arrived just in time to see the side door into the kitchen quarters closing. She gave it a split second before turning the big metal knob and letting herself into the dark passage. She could hear the cook's voice in the kitchen at the far end of the corridor, chastising one of the maids. The knowledge that there were other people about gave her more confidence.

The intruders seemed to have vanished, but the stench of them still filled the narrow corridor. Wenna struggled to keep her stomach from retching. She put a hand over her mouth and waited, listening. Had they gone up the narrow staircase to the main house? Were they holding a knife to her grandmother's throat at this very moment? Wenna shivered. Should she alert the servants, or should she creep upstairs on her own now?

She got halfway up the stone steps when she heard the gruff male voices from the landing above. They didn't sound as if they were in her grandmother's room, but then they wouldn't know where to find that — unless of course this wasn't the first time they had been to Boscawen House.

Wenna's heart quickened as she crept along the corridors. The intruders were nowhere to be seen, but she knew they were there . . . hiding somewhere in the shadows, perhaps. She kept going until the voices, more muffled this time, reached her. Hardly daring to breathe, she followed their direction and then froze, staring at the door of a room that was reserved for guests. The creatures were inside — inside with her grandmother!

Wenna waited for a second, unsure what to do. She listened, but Lady Catherine wasn't calling out for help. She put her ear to the door. Her grandmother's voice was faint, but she didn't sound afraid. She sounded angry. She was chastising the rogues for being late.

Late? Wenna's brow wrinkled. Had these reprobates come here by appointment? Had her grandmother invited them? Her thoughts filtered back to other odd-looking visitors she'd seen at the house. Who were these awful people? Why did they come to her home? Why were they here now? Her head was full of questions. She glanced back along the corridor to reassure herself that no others were lurking in the shadows, and pressed her ear to the door again.

'I told you not to come before dark. You could have been seen. Why do I have to deal with such idiots?'

'We came when we could. No one saw us. We came around the back just as you told us — '

'Be silent, you insolent creature! How dare you answer me back! If I can't trust you to follow my orders, then I will find those who can.'

Wenna heard the rustle of silk and knew her grandmother had got up and was striding across the room. Why were these two not standing up to her? Wenna frowned, not sure what was going on. She heard one of the men give a rasping cough.

'We'll do the job like we always do. Just tell us what you want.'

Job? Wenna frowned. What job? What business did her grandmother have with these unsavoury people?

'The *Southern Star* will be on her way back from France tomorrow. She will have a valuable cargo.'

'And you want us to relieve her of that?'

Wenna's eyes rounded in astonishment. Surely she must have misheard. Why was her grandmother telling these awful men about Mr Luscombe's valuable cargo? The man's rasping laugh made Wenna's blood run cold.

'I want you to do more than that.' Lady Catherine cut him off. 'I have it on good authority that a chest full of gold will be on board the *Southern Star*.'

'Gold, you say?'

'Gold,' her grandmother repeated.

'Gold will cost more,' the man said.

Wenna heard the old woman's stick whacking down on the table. 'It is I who says how much you will be paid, Boskano. You are not in a position to make demands.' A pause, and then: 'And don't think you can raid this ship and cut me out. I have friends — friends who would be more than happy to step into your disgusting shoes. And these particular friends would care nothing about leaving your bloodied, evil-smelling carcasses in the dark filth of the harbour.'

Wenna shuddered. Had her grandmother just threatened to have these rascals murdered if they didn't carry out a raid on an innocent cargo vessel? A shard of ice shot through her. These people were pirates! But even worse, they seemed to be working for her grandmother!

She was fighting hard to keep the swell of nausea in the pit of her stomach from taking over. Boscawen House was entertaining pirates. And from what she had just heard, her grandmother was not only condoning the horrible activities — she was running them!

Wenna reached out to steady herself. Her mind was racing. What could she do? Should she tell someone? But who? Judging by the mutterings from inside the room, the meeting was over. She looked around for a hiding place as the doors opened and pressed herself into a dark corner, holding her breath when the stench of the men reached her as they lumbered past.

Had her grandmother suggested inviting the Plymouth ship-owner and his wife to dine at Boscawen with the sole intention of gleaning information from them? Wenna remembered the pleasant, smiling Sarah Luscombe, and how trusting she had been. She took a long, shuddering breath. That trust had been misplaced. The look that had passed between her grandmother and stepmother when they learned about the gold was filling her head.

She had an instant to make a decision. If she didn't follow these men now, she would have no idea where they went — and she needed to find out what ship they were from if she was to have any chance of stopping this evil. No matter which way they crept away from the house, they were sure to end up on the road to the harbour. If she hurried she could get there ahead of them.

Wenna raced through the house and down the central staircase, letting herself out by the front door. It was dark, so she could run along the main drive without being seen. She drew back when she reached the gates. She could feel her heart pumping as she hid amongst the rhododendron bushes. At first she thought she had missed them; that perhaps they had left the grounds by another means. And then she heard them.

Two shapes appeared out of the darkness. They were grumbling to each other, one of them describing the way in which he would like to 'shut her ladyship up'. Wenna cringed. How could her grandmother have involved herself with these people? But then, how could she do what she was doing at all? The Luscombes had seemed like good and kind people, and yet she planned to rob them.

A thought filtered through Wenna's mind that perhaps the conversation she had just overheard had actually been some kind of trap that her grandmother had been setting to catch these devils. Perhaps she was working on the side of good all along. She did, after all, go to church every Sunday, and the Reverend Osbody often came to take tea.

But as Wenna followed the men back in the direction of the harbour, she knew she had not been mistaken. These people were pirates — and they were working under instruction from Lady Catherine Quintrell.

The salty, tarry smell of the harbour reached Wenna before she got there. The sound of bawdy laughter came from the alehouse on the corner. Just ahead she could see the flickering lamps on the quayside. She had expected that the men she was trailing would amble onto the harbour and board their ship, so their sudden stop took her by surprise. She stepped into the shadows as they turned and looked around before entering the hostelry.

Wenna sank back against a damp wall and sighed. They could be in there for hours, and it certainly wasn't a place she could enter, not even dressed like she was in her dark doublet and cap. Her efforts had been wasted. How would she discover their vessel now?

What was it her grandmother had called one of them? Boskano! She wasn't even sure it was a name. It could have been a derogatory term. She remembered how angry her grandmother had been with them. Would anyone on the quayside recognize the name? No, she couldn't chance just asking. Her stomach rumbled, reminding her that breakfast was the only thing she had eaten that day.

Had it been only yesterday when she'd gone back to the churchyard at Mellin Cove? So much had happened since then. A memory of the moment in the churchyard floated into her mind. She could see Hal kneeling by the new grave, and remembered the softness in his eyes. Why did thoughts of this man keep coming into her head? She didn't know him, and he didn't know her. So why?

She could picture her family around the dining table about now. Her father would be worried that she wasn't there. He would be pacing the floor, perhaps even sending a servant out to look for her. Her stepmother, Margaret, probably wouldn't care one way or the other. But Wenna was in no doubt about her grandmother's feelings. Lady Catherine would be extremely irritated by her absence.

It was something she would have to deal with later. There would be explanations to be made, and she would have to think of something before she arrived home. She was determined that her efforts to find the pirate ship would not be in vain.

The rain was falling in a steady drizzle by the time she reached the quay. The flickering lamps revealed a forest of swaying masts. Her gaze travelled over the ships that were moored along the quayside. Was one of these the pirate ship? How would she know? She could hardly ask anyone.

It was then that the familiar gruff voice reached her. She turned, stepping onto a coiled rope, and almost lost her balance. Heart pounding, she ducked into a shadowy corner and held her breath as the two men who had been with her grandmother earlier stumbled into view. They hadn't been in the alehouse long enough to get drunk, yet they certainly seemed the worse for too much ale. By the looks of them they had spent a great deal of the day partaking in what the hostelry offered.

Wenna shrank further into her corner, watching them make their unsteady way along the quayside. Where were they going? She would never find out if she stayed hiding in this corner. Cautiously she stepped back out onto the glistening cobbles. The pair ahead were making slow progress, so it was easy to keep up with them. Wenna decided that they were so inebriated that they probably would not even notice she was following them. She was close now . . . close enough to catch what they were saying.

'I want you up with t'lark, Billy Nance. The *Blessed Huntress* won't be sailing without a crew. We 'ave to find 'em, and you baint do that lying in yous pit.'

The smaller man looked up, giving his companion a toothless grin. 'Aye,

Capt'n Abel. I'll no be letting yous down.'

Captain Abel Boskano threw an arm drunkenly over Nance's shoulder. 'Yous be a good man, Nance. Best first mate a skipper could 'ave.'

They had reached the end of the quay and stopped, swaying, in front of a dark ship, its rigging towering high into the night sky. Wenna watched as both men clambered aboard, only daring to breathe when they had disappeared down below. She stared after them. What was she supposed to do now? She glanced around, but there was no one in sight. Judging by the noise emanating earlier from the alehouse, they were probably all inside.

This end of the harbour was dark. She shivered at how sinister it felt. She now knew the name of their ship, the *Blessed Huntress*. It was time to go home; time to work out how she would explain to her family where she had been all day.

Any thought of slipping quietly into

Boscawen House while the family dined was immediately dashed as soon as she crept in through the servants' entrance. Mrs Sproggit, the cook, had been listening for her and waddled out from the kitchen, a wooden spoon in her hand.

'The Master wants to see you, Miss Rowenna . . . straight away.'

Wenna swallowed. 'Is he is very angry?' The question was irrelevant, because she knew how displeased her father would be.

'He be waiting dinner for you. The family is in the drawing room and none of them's looking too happy.'

Wenna turned tail and took off up the back stairs, racing to her bedchamber to change into a gown. Seeing her dressed in her present clothes would only further ignite her father's anger.

Her grandmother and stepmother would have ordered her to bed without any dinner, but she wouldn't actually have minded that as much as the impending confrontation with her father. She knew she was a disappointment to him, and that saddened her.

The three of them were waiting in the drawing room. Her father stood in front of the fire, hands clutching the lapels of his wine-coloured velvet jacket, his face puce with annoyance. Her stepmother sat to one side of the fire, an irritated expression on her face. Wenna was aware of the straight-backed figure of her grandmother occupying the opposite chair, but she deliberately avoided her disdainful stare. She wondered how haughty the Lady Catherine would be if the others knew of her treachery.

Wenna kept her head down, but her cheeks flamed as her father's torrent of angry words flowed over her. Sir George was still red-faced when they went in to dine, but the two women were looking distinctly pleased with themselves, and Wenna knew they had enjoyed the little scene.

Wenna had no appetite for food, not even for Mrs Sproggit's delicious crown of beef; but she did her best, pushing it around her plate with her cutlery to give the impression that she was eating.

The end of the meal came as a welcome relief. When the dessert plates had been cleared, Wenna asked if she might be excused. After a fleeting glance to the women, her father nodded. Her ordeal was at an end.

The contorted evil face of the pirate Boskano floated in and out of her dreams that night. Wenna saw vessels, their decks swilling in blood, their sails ripped to tatters, and their crews screaming in agony.

# 5

There had been an atmosphere in the kiddley that night. Annie said nothing, but Enor was sure she knew something of his plans. The place seemed to empty after dark, which was unusual since this was the time most customers normally started to arrive.

'You might as well have a break, Enor,' Annie said. 'Looks like being a quiet night.'

So Enor had gone back to the cottage. It was dark, but something was different. He stared around the harbour. Where were the boats? The fishing fleet had gone! He tried to remember the last time he'd seen the luggers tied up by the quay, but he wasn't sure.

He stood for a moment, gazing up at the dark outline of Mellin Hall. He could just make out lamps glowing at some of the windows. A buzz of excitement swept through him. He'd waited a long time for this, and now his chance had come.

What he wanted to do more than anything was to march up to the towering oak door of Mellin Hall and pull on that great bell. He could imagine a maid, frowning at the late hour, scurrying to see who this visitor was. He saw himself sweeping into the great hall and issuing instructions for the maid to fetch her master.

He'd gone over this in his head so many times. What he would say . . . how he would say it. There could be no faltering. It had to be right . . . But maybe not just yet. He gazed up at the Hall's impressive stone façade and felt a jolt of excitement shoot through him. Dangerous! He would have to temper his enthusiasm for just a bit longer.

Enor didn't sleep that night. His goal was almost in sight, and at first light he would put his plan into action.

* * *

Wenna woke with a start next morning, her night clothes wringing with perspiration. She struggled to sit up in bed. It had been a bad dream. For a second, relief flooded over her, and then the realization dawned. The terrible images of her dream were exactly what was going to happen to the poor *Southern Star* unless she did something to stop it.

She considered telling her father what she had overheard, but would he believe her? She doubted it. She hardly believed it herself.

Her father had left early for London, so only her grandmother and stepmother were at the breakfast table when she went down. The conversations were formal; it seemed that no one was in a mood for talking that morning — a situation that suited Wenna just fine.

She had an idea, but she needed advice. She would go to the one person she trusted — and that meant returning to Mellin Cove. Annie would know what to do.

Her grandmother and stepmother

were keeping a suspicious eye on her, so there was no chance of changing back into the breeches she felt most comfortable in. This time she wouldn't sneak out of the house. She would leave with her head high — with or without her grandmother's approval. Slipping her long woollen cloak over her dark green gown, she picked up her sketchbook and went to say goodbye to them.

Lady Catherine slipped her spectacles down her nose and scowled over them. 'So, young lady, just where do you think you're off to?'

Wenna cast her eyes down demurely, hoping it would be seen as a ladylike gesture while she worked out what to say. She decided to throw caution to the wind and tell the truth. 'I thought to visit the Rosens. They live just a short walk away.'

Lady Catherine frowned. 'The Rosens? You mean those people who were our servants? Why in heaven's name would you want to do that?'

'Annie was my friend,' Wenna protested. 'And I would like to see her again.' She paused. 'I believe she will want me to stay the night, so don't expect me home.'

Her grandmother was on her feet. 'I give no such permission. You most certainly will not spend the night with these people.' Her eyes blazed with anger. 'In fact, I am confining you to your room.' She reached for a hand bell by her side and shook it vigorously. Seconds later her butler Henry Blewitt appeared, puffing.

'Lady Rowenna is unwell, Blewitt. Please take her to her room — and make sure she stays there. Lock the door if you have to.'

Wenna was pink with fury. How dare her grandmother treat her like this?

Blewitt gave her an uneasy glance.

'Can I trust you to do that, Blewitt?' Lady Catherine's voice rose with impatience.

The butler swallowed. 'Of course, your ladyship.' He turned to Wenna.

'Lady Rowenna, allow me to help you.' He reached out to take Wenna's arm, but she snatched it away. She thought about pushing the man aside and sweeping past him right out the front door, but what would that achieve? None of this was his fault. She had to calm down and work out what to do next.

* * *

Back at Mellin Cove, Enor's heart was pumping wildly as he took the steep path from the harbour up to the big house. The servants' entrance was not difficult to find; not as grand as the one the St Neots used, but it would hardly be that. He crossed the yard, heading for the small wooden door in the corner.

He almost didn't see the animal in time. Suddenly it was bolting towards him, head rearing in panic. Enor's first instinct was to save himself; to dive out of the horse's frantic flight. He had no idea what caused him to hurl himself on the beast. For a few terrifying seconds they wrestled each other, the horse more frightened than wild. And then Enor made a grab for the mane, speaking gently all the time to settle and calm the animal.

Gradually the wild rearing ceased and the horse was still. A man appeared from a stable door and came running towards them, a harness in his hand. He threw it over the horse's head. 'Easy, Pegasus . . . easy, boy,' he said.

The horse snorted and pawed at the ground, but the panic had subsided. The man took a deep breath. 'I don't know who you are, but I owe you a debt of gratitude.' He offered Enor his hand. 'I'm Tomas Sweet, and I reckon you've just saved Pegasus's life.'

Enor gave him a cheeky grin. 'He's a frisky one all right, but it was nothing. Anybody would have done the same.'

'I'm not so sure. Not everyone knows how to handle horses. What's your name, lad?'

'Enor Vingoe, sir.'

'What's your business here, Enor Vingoe?'

'I'm looking for work, sir. I was just about to enquire in the kitchen if there was anything going. I'm prepared to wash pots . . . scrub floors . . . anything.'

Tomas scratched his head. 'Don't reckon they'll be needing no more floor scrubbers over there, but I might have something for you.'

Enor smiled. It wasn't what he'd planned, but it looked like things were going his way. He tilted his head inquisitively and waited for the man to go on.

'Come into the stables, lad,' Tomas said, walking ahead of him and leading Pegasus back to his stall. There were four other horses in the stables, two of them black stallions that eyed him with caution. The others were concentrating on munching their way through their hay bales.

'I'm guessing you know about horses,'

Tomas said, stroking Pegasus's mane, and focusing on keeping the horse calm as he settled him back into his stall. 'Tell me where you worked before.'

Enor was thinking on his feet. Should he admit that he knew nothing about horses; that the only horse he'd ever known was the aged mare his father had used to work the meagre plot of land he farmed over Helston way?

He cleared his throat. 'Boskilly House near Helston.' It was the first thing he'd thought of. A lad from his village had gone to work on that estate. He knew the family's name was Tregothen, but that was it. He was relying on this man having no more knowledge than he had himself about that family. He swallowed, waiting.

'And you worked in the stables at Boskilly?' Tomas asked.

Enor nodded. 'I like horses. I get on with them.'

'So why did you leave?'

Another tricky question. He took a breath. 'My father was ill. I was needed at home.' He paused, his mind whirring. He had to get this right. The man could check this bit. It wasn't exactly a lie; his father had been ill, but not as seriously as he'd made out. He had talked him into persuading his aunt Annie to let him stay with her and Jory in Mellin Cove for a while. He needed to be here if his plan was to work. The couple might be his great aunt and uncle, but they were nothing to him. He didn't know them. He had no feelings for them. When he had what rightly belonged to him, he wouldn't need them anymore.

'That doesn't explain what you're doing here in Mellin Cove,' Tomas said.

Enor caught his breath and explained about the Rosens, making sure the man noticed the lump in his throat when he described how good they had been to him.

Tomas pursed his lips and nodded. 'I was impressed with what you did out there, young Enor. How do you feel about mucking out?'

Enor cocked an eyebrow.

'Don't go thinking you'll be making your fortune here; but if you want the work, and you're prepared to put your back into it, then there's a place here for you . . . if you want it, that is.'

'I've never run from hard work, sir,' Enor said. 'And I won't be starting now. I'm very pleased to accept your kind offer.'

It was another hour before Kit St Neot strode into the stables. Tomas had saddled one of the black stallions, and gave a broad smile when he saw his master. 'I've got Sabre all ready for you, Master Kit.'

Kit returned the smile. 'No wind today, Tomas. It's a fine morning for a gallop across the moors.' He glanced across at Enor. 'Who's this?'

'My new stable lad, sir. Enor Vingoe. His aunt and uncle run the kiddley down at the cove.'

Kit turned with interest. 'Didn't I see you at Sam Pentreath's funeral? Did you know Sam?'

'I didn't, sir. My great aunt and uncle couldn't be there, so I went in their stead. It was what they wanted.'

'So you're Annie and Jory's great nephew?'

Enor, gripping his brush with one hand and touching his forehead in a gesture of subservience with the other, nodded. 'They've been so good to me, sir. This job means I can repay some of that kindness.'

'Where are you from, Enor?'

'Over Helston way, sir. My father felt I needed to spread my wings, so to speak.'

'So the Rosens took you under their roof?' Kit guessed.

'Just until I get myself sorted and find a place of my own, sir.'

Kit gave him a thoughtful nod before turning to mount his horse. Enor leaned on his brush, his top lip curling in distain as he stared after horse and rider. That place of his own would come sooner than Kit St Neot knew . . . sooner than any of them at Mellin

Cove knew. A slow smile crept over his face. Enor Vingoe's fortunes were about to change.

* * *

It was hours before Wenna's anger had subsided. She'd considered ripping the drapes from her bed and tying them together to form a rope to lower herself from the window, but decided against it. What would that achieve if she fell and broke her neck? No, she had to be patient. Not even her grandmother could keep her a prisoner forever. Her father would have something to say about this when he heard.

Lunchtime came and went and Wenna was offered no meal. Was her grandmother planning to starve her into submission?

It was early evening before the door opened and her stepmother appeared. 'Well?' she demanded, pulling herself up to her full five foot three inches. 'Have we learned our lesson?'

Wenna longed to throw back an indignant retort, but that would come later. For the moment she would go along with whatever little game the two women were playing. She hung her head and nodded.

Her stepmother smiled. 'In that case, your grandmother says you may come down for dinner, which under the circumstances I think is very generous.'

Wenna followed Margaret down the stairs and into the dining room, where Lady Catherine sat at the head of the table. She inclined her head towards a chair, indicating that Wenna should sit.

Her stepmother seated herself opposite. The meal was conducted in total silence. Only when the last plates were removed did her grandmother speak. 'It does not pay for a young lady to be so high-spirited. It is time you learned decorum. Do you understand, Rowenna?'

Wenna nodded.

'Just make sure of that,' her stepmother interrupted. 'We are both watching you, Rowenna, and we are not liking what we see. You may be able to twist your father around your little finger, but your grandmother and I see you differently.'

Wenna could feel her temper rising. She itched to stand up for herself, but now was not the time, so she said nothing. She could feel their eyes on her as she left the room.

When she entered her bedchamber, the first thing she saw was the key on her dressing table. So, the indignity of having been locked up all day was over. Did the two women downstairs really believe they could control her so easily? She snatched up the key and clutched it to her chest, smiling. Her visit to Annie would be a little later than she'd planned, but she was definitely going.

Wenna gathered up her things and locked the door after her. With a little luck no one would check on her before morning. She crept down the stairs and slipped silently out of the house, feeling a little light-headed as she ran down the drive. Getting out of Boscawen without anyone noticing had been easier than she'd thought.

There was no moon, but she knew the terrain over the moors well enough not to trip and fall in the darkness. In the distance she could make out the lights of Mellin Hall, and ahead to her right she could see candles flickering in the Rev Collett's home. It helped her to judge where the turning would be for the cove. She could hear the breakers crashing at the bottom of the cliffs as she made her way down the path that led to the harbour.

Annie had told her that she once lived in a cottage down here. She just had to find the right one. She stared into the darkness. The little row of white stone dwellings was just visible. Should she knock on every door? Her eye was taken to the far side of the harbour, and to lights twinkling there. She could hear voices; men laughing. It seemed to be some kind of alehouse, and yet not raucous like the place at

Boscawen Harbour. She had expected to see fishing boats in the harbour, but the place looked deserted.

She had no idea if Annie would welcome a visit from her after all this time. She began to feel a little knot of doubt in her stomach. Maybe this had not been such a good idea after all. But she was here now, and she had no intention of turning back.

She knocked on one of the doors, and when a woman answered she explained she was looking for the Rosens, and was directed to the end cottage beside the alehouse. At her first knock Annie appeared. Even at this late hour she was wiping floury hands on her apron. The kindly blue eyes crinkled and she let out a yell of recognition, throwing her arms wide to gather Wenna into them.

'My dear girl, how wonderful to see you. What brings you to Mellin Cove — and so late?'

Wenna sniffed in the delicious smell of baking and submitted herself to

Annie's enthusiastic hug. 'It's a long story. Can I save it for later?'

Annie narrowed her eyes. 'Are you in some kind of trouble, child?'

'I'm absolutely fine.' Wenna laughed. 'I should have come to see you sooner. I don't know why I haven't.'

'Well, that matters nothing, my dear, because you're here now, and right pleased I am to see you.'

A large brown enamel kettle was put to boil; and as she waited for their tea, Wenna settled back, enjoying the pleasure of being in Annie's company again.

'I did think to come visit some time back when I came upon that big funeral up in the churchyard,' Wenna said. 'I was surprised that you and Jory were not there. It seemed like every man, woman and child from these parts had turned up.'

Annie nodded. 'Sam Pentreath. Such a tragedy. A young man cut down in his prime. Jory and I were away then, or we would have been there.'

Wenna frowned, remembering Hal and the rest of the man's grown-up family. He couldn't have been that young; but then neither was Annie.

'We have a visitor staying with us at the moment,' Annie explained. 'Enor is the son of my nephew, Peder. He insisted on going to Sam's burial in our place.'

'I never heard you mention an Enor before,' Wenna said.

Annie got up and went to the oven, catching a cloth to slide out the tray of bread. She came back to the table and plonked herself down, cheeks pink from the heat of the oven. She shook her head. 'Such a troubled boy.'

'Enor?'

'He's about your age, Rowenna; perhaps a bit older. Never settled to anything. Such a worry for Peder and Rebecca.' She gave a long sigh. 'Anyway, Jory and I agreed to have him here in Mellin Cove for a few weeks just to give all of them a break. We didn't think he would come, but he seemed more than keen. He's still here.'

# 6

Jem glanced along the heaving deck of the *Sally P* at the three bodies stretched out in the bow. A concerned frown creased his brow. 'How are they, Daniel?' he shouted.

'This one's coming round but the other two are still out cold,' Daniel yelled back, ringing out a wet rag and placing it on the bloody forehead of one of the injured men.

'Can't be far from the coast, Skipper,' Sal Carney hollered out against the driving rain. 'We be'ome soon.'

Jem drew the back of his hand across his wet face and nodded. And not before time, he thought. He wasn't sure how long his injured passengers would cling to life. That was, if all of them were still living. Two of the men looked more dead than alive. He glanced up into the dark night at the billowing sail. At least the wind was strong and gave no sign of subsiding. By his reckoning, another two hours should see them back in harbour.

Across to his right, he could make out the shape of the *Bright Star* powering through the waves; its skipper, Pascow Hendry, at the helm. He had pulled on board two more survivors from the wreck of the *Southern Star*. Jem knew there was no point in trying to call across to him. Any shout would be lost in this weather.

The rest of the Mellin Cove fleet was scattered further out to sea. He wished they were heading home in daylight. The red sails of the luggers would have been a comforting sight. As it was, he could only hope that they were somewhere close. He had no idea if these boats had managed to rescue anyone, but he dearly hoped so.

Across the deck, Sal's father Daniel had raised his arm. 'Another of 'em's comin' round,' he called out.

Jem shouted to Sal, indicating he should take the helm. When control of the lugger had been safely transferred, Jem made his way along the deck and crouched down beside the casualties. One of them looked to have some authority. 'Can you tell me your name?' he asked.

The man heaved himself up on his elbows. 'William Colby . . . Captain William Colby.' He extended a trembling hand, which Jem took.

'I'm Jem Pentreath.' He nodded to his crewmen. 'This is Daniel Carney and his son, Sal.' He paused. 'I'm sorry about your ship. Was your cargo very valuable?'

The man did not respond, but whether from reluctance or sheer exhaustion, Jem didn't know. He narrowed his eyes into the wind and stared out at the black sea. Pirates didn't usually target such vessels. Pickings were thin. Gold and gems, bolts of silks and kegs of brandy — these things were more in their line.

Captain Colby struggled round to where he could see his two injured crewmen. He shook his head. 'Those devils will pay for what they did.' He looked up at Jem. 'How many others survived?'

'I'm not sure,' Jem said, nodding towards the lugger sailing alongside them. 'The *Bright Star* has two, and I think I saw others being dragged aboard the *Good Bess* and the *Cornish Bounty*.' His shoulders lifted in a shrug. 'After that . . . '

Captain Colby swallowed, and Jem could see the man was struggling with his emotions. He put a hand on his shoulder. 'We should be landing in less than an hour. We'll know a bit more then about your crew.'

'Thank you. We owe you such a debt of gratitude.'

Jem grimaced. 'I'm just sorry we couldn't save your ship. What line was she from?'

'The Luscombes of Plymouth.'

'Luscombe, you say?'

The man gave a weak nod. 'Are you familiar with the family?'

Jem was. 'My brother-in-law's wife, Dewi, is a Luscombe. I've met her father, Richard.'

Colby hung his head and shook it. 'Richard will take this badly. The loss of a ship is a terrible thing.'

'The loss of a crew is a worse one,' Jem commented. 'And if I am any judge of character, Richard Luscombe will be more concerned about that than his ship.'

'You're right of course, but it's still a bad business.'

Jem patted the man's shoulder as he got to his feet and stretched his back as he returned to the helm, instructing Sal to help Daniel look after the injured men.

* * *

Annie had been staring at the window as she and Wenna spoke, and now she jumped up, frowning. 'The lights.' She pointed out to sea.

Wenna went to the window. She could see tiny specks of light out in the darkness.

'Surely this can't be the fleet coming back,' Annie said. 'Not at this time.' She'd gone to stand beside Wenna. She couldn't see the red sails, but it had to be the boats — and they were heading for harbour.

'Perhaps they're coming into shelter from the weather. The wind is getting up out there,' Wenna suggested.

Annie shook her head. 'No, I've seen them out in all kinds of weather. A bit of wind is nothing to them.' She frowned. 'No, something's happened.'

Cold ice was gripping Wenna's insides. 'How far out do they fish?' She could now see the definite shapes of the approaching boats. Surely the fleet's early return could have nothing to do with the *Southern Star*? She was on her way from France. And besides, Boskano had only received his orders from her grandmother the day before.

Nothing could have happened yet.

'Usually they don't go much further than the headland, but I believe they had other duties at this time.'

Wenna's brain was whirring. 'What other duties, Annie?'

'I'm gossiping. Pay no heed to me. It's not my business; I should not have said anything.'

'Do you mean they were smuggling, Annie?'

'Like I said, it's none of my business. I spoke out of turn and I'd be glad if it wasn't repeated.'

'Of course I won't repeat it, but I must know — did the fleet go to France last night?'

Annie's face was all the confirmation she needed. Her hand went to her mouth. Something terrible had happened, she just knew it.

Wenna followed Annie out to the harbour. Other women were gathering there. Obviously Annie was not the only one who was concerned at the unexpectedly early return of the fleet.

They all watched as the vessels approached the mouth of the harbour and sailed in one by one. Wenna glanced along to the end of the quay. There was a man standing there, his hand to his forehead as he peered out at the approaching fleet. Wenna's heart turned over. It was Hal. He was waving to the boats now, indicating where they should tie up.

The woman she'd seen comforting Hal's mother at his father's funeral was running to the harbour, her black cloak flapping at her heels. 'Annie! Do you know what's happened? Why are the boats back?' she called.

'I know no more than you, Hedra, but something's not right.'

* * *

News of the sinking of the *Southern Star* had not reached Mellin Cove as the fishing fleet sailed in, but the gathering of women and children on the quay indicated to Jem that they knew something was wrong. Wives and mothers never quite believed their menfolk would always return safely. Fishing was a dangerous business, and not always as profitable as it might be. This time the luggers had unexpected extra cargo.

Jem scanned the figures on the quay, and his face split into a wide grin when he spotted Hedra. She waved, and he raised his hand in response, his heart quickening as it always did when he caught sight of her. He could see Hal gesturing to the boats, guiding them in.

Captain Colby was now on his feet and standing beside Jem. He nodded out to the quay. 'Your wife?'

'Yes, that's my wife.' The pride in Jem's voice was unmistakable.

The *Sally P* came alongside first, and Hedra ran to meet it. Immediately Wenna saw the injured men on her deck. The other fishing luggers appeared one by one, each boat carrying casualties. The quayside was now milling with people. The words 'pirate attack' rang out above the melee.

Wenna stared in horror at the scene before her. This was Boskano's doing. The *Blessed Huntress* must have sailed that same night she'd followed Boskano and Nance. Could she have stopped it? She didn't know. One thing was sure — there was no way she could admit to these people that her grandmother had been responsible for this.

The women were rushing to greet their menfolk, already aware that something had happened. Jem saw their uncertain expressions turn to shock as they caught sight of the injured members of the *Southern Star*'s crew.

Hedra rushed forward as the *Sally P* drew alongside the quay, a hand clasped to her mouth. 'Whatever's happened? Is everyone all right?' She reached forward to help the tall silver-haired man off the boat. His arm was damaged and there was a nasty gash on his forehead. 'You poor man,' she said, glancing back at the other injured men that Jem and Daniel were helping onto the quay. One of them appeared to be unconscious.

'I have the wagon,' Hal called. 'It's at the top of the hill. I'll fetch it.'

Wenna stared around her in bewilderment. She felt Annie's hand on her shoulder. 'Come with me,' she said. 'There'll be work for us to do.'

The quayside was in turmoil as people rushed back and forth to help the casualties. Someone mentioned the *Southern Star*. Wenna stared in horror as Annie attempted to tug her away. This was her grandmother's doing. She was the one responsible for this nightmare. How else could it be described?

'Help the men on the *Good Bess*,' Annie called back to her as she took off along the quay. 'I'll see what I can do on the *Bounty*.'

Over the melee, Wenna heard someone call out, 'We'll ferry the injured to Mellin Hall. Kit and Dewi have more room to look after them up there.'

Wenna was still struggling to overcome her confusion and feelings of guilt. Why was she still standing here? She needed to help. Some of the walking wounded were beginning to stagger from the boats. She rushed to their aid, guiding the men to the farm wagon that Hal had brought down to the quay. For a brief moment their eyes met as he reached to pull an injured sailor on board. Wenna thought she saw a flicker of recognition in the concerned brown eyes. She glanced up, not daring to smile, as he offered his hand to haul her up onto the wagon.

The injured sailor was whimpering now, and she turned to him, concentrating on comforting the man who now seemed to be in her care.

News of the pirate attack had reached Mellin Hall before Hal's wagon rumbled up with the first of the injured survivors. Kit and Dewi were already rushing across the yard to meet them.

'Captain Colby!' Dewi gasped, her hand flying to her mouth. There was so much blood on the man's face that she almost hadn't recognized him. 'You're hurt. Let me help you.' She put a hand under his elbow, but he waved her away.

'Don't concern yourself with me, Mistress. Attend to the others. I can look after myself.'

She ignored him, supporting his arm as he limped alongside her into the hall. She led him into the great drawing room and gently lowered him onto one of the large oak fireside chairs. The others followed.

'Are you able tell me what happened, Captain?' Her voice was gentle.

'Pirate attack!' The words came in gasps. 'We would all be dead but for your fleet.'

Wenna kept her head down, but on hearing the word 'pirate' it jerked up as her eyes flew open. She mustn't give herself away. She could continue helping these people so long as no one questioned her presence. She mingled with the others in the now crowded room. Everyone was so busy caring for the injured that she would hardly be noticed. If she were lucky, they would assume she was related to one of the village women and would pay no attention to her efforts to help.

Hedra had appeared at Dewi's side, her hand on the hot forehead of the man her sister-in-law was attending to. 'He has a temperature,' she said. 'We need cold flannels.'

'What about the others?' Dewi asked, sending a worried glance over the activities around her. 'Some of those injuries look bad.'

Hedra nodded, the anxiety in her eyes saying it all. 'If you can cope with this one, I'll see what help the others need.'

'We'll be fine here,' Dewi said, looking down at her patient and giving him what she hoped was a reassuring smile. The last time she'd seen this man was in her father's house in Plymouth. Captain Colby and his wife Martha had been dinner guests, and Dewi had taken to the couple immediately. She could see him now, laying down the silver cutlery on his cleared plate and regaling the diners with yet another tale of his exciting sea voyages. Captain Colby was one of her father's most trusted captains, and a good friend. He would be greatly distressed when he learned of this.

She put a hand on the man's shoulder as he struggled to sit up. 'No, don't try to move. You must rest. You've been badly hurt, sir.'

'We must get word to your father.' He winced from the effort of speaking. 'The ship . . . ' He was gasping for breath. She hadn't dared to ask about that. The loss of the *Southern Star* would all but finish her father's business.

'She's gone,' the captain said. 'I couldn't save her.'

Dewi had known what was coming but the shock still hit her, slamming into her head like a herd of wild horses. She could feel the blood drain from her face — but this was no time to indulge in regret. This terrible thing had happened and these men needed her help.

The sea captain touched her shoulder, eyes full of remorse. 'There was nothing I could do. They were on us before we knew.' He lifted his head to stare across to the great mullioned windows and the dark sea beyond. All around him was chaos as the Mellin Hall servants, and the villagers who had rushed up the hill to help them, moved around tending to his injured and traumatized men. But he saw none of this. His mind was filled with the terrible sight of the pirate ship looming up from the stern. In an instant it had been alongside. He could hear the devils yelling obscenities at them; see the flash of their steel as cutlasses were brandished. The foul smell of them assaulted his nostrils as they swarmed aboard the *Southern Star*. Chaos was suddenly everywhere, blades glinted, and bodies were slashed. Yelling and screaming filled the air. The deck of the *Southern Star* was awash with blood. The moans of his injured crewmen filled his head . . .

Dewi put a hand on his shoulder. Captain Colby's eyes were bulging with the memory of the horror he had so recently been a part of. He tried to give himself a shake, forcing himself back into the room. 'I've let them all down,' he said. 'This is my fault.'

But Dewi shushed him into silence. 'You couldn't possibly have foreseen this. The Channel is a dangerous place.'

'Still . . . it was my responsibility to keep my crew and ship safe.' He shook his head. He had never lost a vessel before.

'Are all your crew here?' Dewi asked gently. 'Is anyone missing?'

Colby glanced around the room. Bodies were strewn everywhere, while those tending them went from one to the other, carrying bowls of steaming water and ripping up sheets as makeshift dressings. He made a quick head count — eight men. Three were missing.

Jesemy appeared at their side, setting a jug of water on the table and dipping a clean rag into it. 'Let me clean this one up, Mistress.' She cocked her head to one side and gave him an understanding look.

But Dewi took the wet rag from her. 'It's fine, thank you, Jesemy. I can attend to the captain.' She nodded across the room. 'You have enough to do.'

'I have a big pot of chicken broth simmering on the hob. Reckon it won't go wrong. Some of these poor souls look as if they haven't had a square meal in some time.'

Dewi smiled. 'I'm sure that would be very welcome, Jesemy.' The servant gave the captain an uncertain look before returning to her tasks in the kitchen.

# 7

Wenna was also in the kitchen, helping Jesemy's husband Tomas to fill jugs of warm water to bathe the men's wounds. She was struggling with a particularly heavy vessel when Hal appeared by her side. He took it from her. 'You shouldn't put so much water in them,' he said.

She flushed, but when she looked up he was turning away. She could see he was smiling. She watched his easy stride as he went back to the makeshift hospital in the drawing room. Her knees were shaking as she followed him through and saw him go round filling bowls. He hadn't said anything about recognizing her, yet she was sure that he had.

She tore her eyes away from Hal and glanced around the room. Things were beginning to look more organized.

Across the way she could see Annie on her knees beside a poor man whose expression showed he was in great pain. Annie looked up and spotted Wenna and waved her over.

'This man has a dislocated shoulder. I need your help, Wenna. Can you hold him down while I pull it back into place?'

Wenna knelt by the man and gave him a reassuring smile. The whole process sounded grim, but she followed Annie's instructions, wincing as the man yelled out in pain while his shoulder clicked back into place. She looked at Annie in amazement. 'Where did you learn to do that?'

Annie smiled down at her patient, who was giving a relieved sigh. 'My mother was a wise old owl,' she said.

Kit caught Jem's eye and crossed the room to him. 'What happened, man? These poor devils look like they are on their last legs.' He frowned back to where Dewi was gently dabbing Captain Colby's bloodied brow. 'Is it true that this was a Luscombe ship?'

'I'm afraid so.' Jem sighed. 'Not exactly good news for you and Dewi.'

'No . . . This will hit Dewi's father hard. No one can afford to lose a ship. I don't know if Luscombe Shipping can bear the loss.'

'You mean the company could fail?' Jem was shocked.

'It's a possibility.' Kit sighed into the silence. 'I'll send someone to Plymouth with the news; but knowing Richard Luscombe, he will be more concerned about these poor souls.'

'Do you think he will come to Mellin Cove?'

'Undoubtedly.' He glanced back to Dewi, who was now wrapping a dressing around Captain Colby's head.

'Have you any idea who did this?' Kit asked.

Jem's expression was grim. 'The ship was the *Blessed Huntress*.'

Kit stared at him. 'You know this ship, Jem?'

'I'm not sure . . . maybe.'

'Maybe?'

'I've seen it before, though it was under different circumstances.'

Kit continued looking at him, his silence urging Jem on.

'We were on a trip to Cherbourg.' Jem glanced around to make sure he was not being overheard. 'It wasn't a fishing trip.'

Kit nodded. 'I understand.'

'The *Blessed Huntress* came into harbour — and half the harbour population disappeared.'

'You will have to explain that to me. I don't understand.'

'They were all afraid of the *Blessed Huntress* — or more accurately, her captain Abel Boskano. Much as I detest to say so, the man is Cornish.'

'Really?' Kit was trying to digest this.

'He's been seen around Falmouth.'

'Really? By who?'

'By me. I only caught a glimpse of the creature as they turned tail, but I'm certain it was the same man.'

'But surely if this *Blessed Huntress* is

a pirate ship, he will have to lie low?'

'That would be no problem, Kit. You know as well as I do that Cornwall is full of secret creeks and coves; he would have no trouble disappearing.'

Kit nodded. 'We need a plan if we are to hunt down this ship and her evil master.'

Jem was frowning. 'There is a puzzle about this whole business. The *Southern Star* was not carrying a valuable cargo. According to Captain Colby, her hold was less than half-full and contained only timber. Apparently business was slow in the French ports. The ships' captains were vying with each other for cargo.'

'Boskano would not have known that, though, would he?'

'I believe he did know. He must have seen that the *Southern Star* sat high in the water, an obvious sign that she carried no significant cargo. The man may be a murdering devil, but I don't believe he is stupid.'

'So why? If it wasn't the cargo he was

after, why did he attack an innocent ship? And from what you say, he didn't simply want to capture it, otherwise why would he sink her?'

'I can think of only one reason,' Jem said grimly. 'He was working under the orders of someone else . . . someone who, for whatever reason, wanted the *Southern Star* sunk. I can think of only one reason why anyone would do that. I believe the real target was Richard Luscombe.'

Kit's eyes narrowed as the implication of what Jem had just said sank in. He blinked. 'You mean Boskano thought Richard was on board?'

'Not necessarily. There are many ways to destroy a man — or his business.'

'They sank the *Southern Star* to damage Luscombe Shipping? But why?'

Jem shrugged. 'That's what I don't know. I think you need to talk with your father-in-law, Kit. Someone needs to warn him.'

Kit nodded, but his eyes were on the

young woman tending to a wounded crewman on the far side of the room. She wasn't from the village. He turned to ask Jem who she was, but Hedra was waving Jem over to help lift a particularly heavy seaman.

Kit walked across to where Dewi was tying a dressing around Captain Colby's damaged wrist. 'How's the patient?' He smiled down at the man.

'I have a good nurse.' Captain Colby flashed an appreciative smile to Dewi.

'You're not the only one by all accounts.' Kit glanced across to where Wenna was winding a long strip of rag around a gash in the arm of another casualty. 'I didn't realize you had a passenger.'

Captain Colby followed Kit's gaze and frowned. 'I had no passenger.'

'I'm assuming she was not one of your crew . . . a stowaway, perhaps?'

Colby shook his head. 'Not possible. I always order a search of the ship before we leave a port. What makes you think the young lady was on my ship?'

Kit shrugged. If she didn't come from the *Southern Star*, then . . . ?

But just as he spoke, Annie Rosen crossed the room to put an arm around the girl and lowered her head to speak in her ear. Jory must have arrived at some point because he was moving towards the two women.

Of course. He smiled. She must have been visiting Annie and Jory. It made sense now.

Hal had also been watching Wenna. He almost hadn't recognized her as the one who drew pictures in the field of stones. Always before, she had been dressed like a boy. But once he had noticed the long tendril of pale hair that had escaped from her cap and had almost smiled and nodded to her that day, though he had checked himself. He had no wish to frighten her.

But now she looked up, and it was she who was smiling. She was crossing the room to him. His heart began to pound.

'It *is* you, isn't it?' she said, looking

up at him. 'I've seen you pass by in the lane with your horse.'

Hal cleared his throat. 'You're the one who does the drawing.' It was a ridiculous thing to say, but he felt awkward. He wasn't comfortable with women, especially ones as young as this.

Wenna put a hand to her head. There was a smear of blood on her cheek.

'Here,' he said, turning to the table next to him and dipping a clean strip of dressing in a bowl of water. 'You have a smear on your cheek.'

'Oh, I didn't know.' She raised her fingers to her face. 'I can't see. Will you wipe it clean for me?' She couldn't believe she was being so forward. She hoped he couldn't see how much she was trembling.

Hal squeezed out the excess water and drew the wet rag across her cheek. He didn't like how much the young woman's closeness was disturbing him. 'I have the wagon outside if you need to be escorted home,' he said curtly.

'What makes you think I need to be escorted? I can look after myself, you know.'

Hal raised an eyebrow. What an ungrateful child. He didn't have to offer to help her. He was about to tell her so when Jem called him from across the room. He and Hedra were taking two of the injured seamen back to Penhalow and needed Hal's wagon.

When Hal turned back, the woman had gone.

# 8

Wenna was furious with herself as she trailed back to Boscawen House. It was almost dawn, and here she was out on the moors all by herself again. Annie had offered her a bed for the night, but Wenna had refused, saying a carriage was coming to collect her. It wasn't true, but she knew there was no way Annie and Jory would have let her walk the moors on her own at this hour.

Hal had offered to escort her home, and she had behaved like a spoiled child. In fact, she had been downright rude to him and she had no idea why, other than that he seemed to be treating her like she was twelve years old and not her actual eighteen years.

By the time she reached Boscawen the sun was rising, and Wenna had never felt so exhausted in her life. She hoped no one had discovered that she'd left the house. All she wanted was to strip off her clothes and collapse into bed. She let herself in by a back door that she knew would not be locked and felt in the pocket of her cloak for the key to her bedchamber.

At first she thought she had imagined the voices as she crept past the door to the morning room. She stopped, holding her breath. Definitely voices. She put her eye to the keyhole and almost cried out in shock at what she saw there.

'Well . . . is she sunk?' Lady Catherine's black eyes glittered with excitement.

'That's just what she be.' Abel Boskano gave a rasping laugh. 'Splinters and firewood down on bed o' Channel — and them that went wi 'er.'

Lady Catherine's head lifted sharply. 'Did many die?'

Boskano's scarred face twisted into an accusing scowl. 'Are you doubting I did your bidding? The crew was spared

— that were your orders, and that be what we did.'

'You did well, Abel. I am pleased.' She stood up and went to a polished rosewood secretaire in the far corner of the room. Taking care to shield what she was doing from her visitor, she put a finger to a concealed button on the side and a compartment slid out. She removed the contents and the compartment slid back.

Boskano's darting, mistrusting eyes never left her as she turned, head high, and walked back to him. She held out the bag containing the gold coins. He snatched at it, ripping back the ties to reveal the gold sovereigns inside.

'It's all there, just as we agreed.' Lady Catherine gave a cold smile.

The man still counted the coins out in his hand. Then he touched his forehead, giving her a sneering grin. 'You are a good and honest woman, your ladyship.'

Wenna had a hand over her mouth to

stop herself from crying out. If she hadn't heard this exchange with her own ears, she would not have believed it. How could her grandmother be so evil?

She needed to share this with her father. Lady Catherine had to be stopped. She had no conscience about what she was doing. Wenna felt a wave of nausea rise up inside her. As far as her grandmother knew, everyone on board that ship could have died, and yet she seemed to be celebrating it. But Wenna would tell people what her grandmother had done . . . what Abel Boskano and his wicked followers had done. They had attacked the crew of the *Southern Star* and left them for dead, and then they had put torches to the ship; and as far as she could see, neither one of them showed an inkling of remorse.

She wished her father was home. He would know what to do. A cold thought was beginning to seep into her brain. What if her father knew about this . . . had even been part of it? She had never suspected her grandmother capable of such evil, but she had been wrong. Could she also be wrong about her father? Had he known about this? The very idea sent a shudder through her.

The exhaustion of a few minutes ago had vanished. Wenna had never felt more awake. She fled to her chamber to collect her thoughts. It was daylight now, and from her window she saw Boskano creep away from the house using the cover of the shrubs around the lawn. She waited until she heard her grandmother's laboured step on the stairs, and then followed her into her bedchamber.

'I know what you did, Grandmother.'

The old woman spun round, and for a split second Wenna saw the fear in the wrinkled face.

'What are you talking about child?'

'I saw Boskano leave. I heard everything.'

'You heard nothing.'

'I will tell Father about your activities.'

'He will not believe you.'

Wenna stepped closer to her grandmother, eyes flaming with threat. 'Oh, I think he will, Grandmother.'

Lady Catherine looked away, restless fingers wringing at her lace handkerchief. 'I was never responsible for any loss of life.' Her bottom lip trembled. 'That was always a stipulation. No one ever died.'

Wenna moved her face closer. 'I don't believe you. How do you know what damage your evil did? You robbed people.'

'I only took from those who could afford to lose it.'

'How can you say that?' Wenna's voice was rising. 'Because your *friends* sacked the *Southern Star*, it may have cost the Luscombes their shipping line.' She turned on her heel and paced the room, wheeling round when she reached the window. 'You have no conception of the damage you have done. You have destroyed people's lives. How could you?'

'I misjudged,' Lady Catherine said quietly. 'I admit that. I was thinking only of relieving those rich French noblemen of their fortunes.'

Wenna frowned. 'How many other men have you relieved of their fortunes?'

Lady Catherine's mouth twitched uncomfortably. 'A few,' she said.

Wenna went on staring at her grandmother. She didn't know the woman at all. She gulped. Her grandmother was a pirate hiding behind the facade of a lady. The more she learned, the more unbelievable the situation became. 'I don't understand. What does a few mean? Are we talking about three? Six? More than six?'

Her grandmother shook her head silently. Sitting there with her shoulders sagging and head bent, there was a look of defeat about her — but even that could not be trusted. Wenna squared up to the old woman. 'What did you do with all that plunder?' Her tone was more controlled than she was feeling.

Lady Catherine raised her head. Had that been a fleeting glimmer of triumph in the dark eyes? 'It's here,' she said.

'What? Here at Boscawen House?' Wenna couldn't hide her shock.

Her grandmother nodded. 'Right here in the anteroom of my bedchamber.'

*The secret room*. Wenna sighed. No one was ever allowed in that room. Well, that was about to change. 'Show me,' she said. 'I want to see inside that room.'

The old lady began to wearily push herself out of her chair. Wenna stepped forward to help her to her feet and then watched her move slowly across the room, hesitating for a moment before the door to the little room.

Wenna's mouth had gone dry. She ran the tip of her tongue over her lips. 'Open this door please, Grandmother.'

Lady Catherine slipped her fingers down the high neck of her gown and drew out a long, fine silver chain. The small key glinted in the morning sunshine that slatted into the bed-chamber. Wenna's heart fluttered with apprehension as her grandmother unlocked the door. She pushed it open and stepped back, an unmistakable expression of excitement in the old lady's eyes.

'This is it. These are my treasures.'

The room was stacked with brass-studded trunks and caskets. Leather and velvet pouches were laid side by side, bulging with their precious contents, and Wenna could see what looked like many silk-covered jewellery boxes.

Her grandmother moved into the room and stood for a moment with her arms outstretched, and then she turned to the caskets, running her fingers reverently over the smooth surface of one of them. She opened a jewellery box and carefully lifted out ropes of gleaming pearls. 'Aren't they beautiful?'

She was in her own little world. Wenna could hardly believe what she was seeing. 'You do know you will have to give all these things back,' she said.

'What?' Her grandmother spun round, her face an expression of total disbelief. 'I'm not giving these things back to anyone. They belong to me now.'

'These things have never belonged to you, Grandmother,' Wenna hit back. 'You stole them, and now you must return them to their rightful owners.'

'And just how do you propose I do that? I have no idea who owned these things before they came to me, or how they came by them.'

Wenna bit her lip, thinking. Her grandmother spoke the truth. How could she return these treasures when she did not even know to whom they had belonged?

'I do have a suggestion though,' Lady Catherine said. 'We could share them. I could give you half of everything in this room. You could be an independently wealthy woman. Not bad for an eighteen-year-old girl.' She stepped closer, eyes gleaming. 'What do you say, Rowenna? You could be rich.'

But another plan was beginning to form in Wenna's mind; a plan she would need some help with. 'You cannot keep any of these things, Grandmother. You must know that. It's not as though you could ever actually wear any of this jewellery.'

'You miss the point, my dear. The pleasure is in the owning of beautiful things, not in displaying them.' She paused. 'You aren't going to tell your father, are you?'

'Not if all these things are moved out of here and you relinquish any interest in them. Those are my conditions. Plus, you must desist from all such illegal activities in the future.' She suddenly had another thought. 'What about my stepmother? What is her involvement in this?'

Her grandmother tutted. 'Margaret has no involvement. The woman is a milksop.'

'But she was aware of your activities?'

'She knew a little. Margaret's tiny mind would never have grasped the magnitude of all this.' She waved a hand around the treasures. 'A few pieces of gold soon silenced her.'

A sudden compassion for her father swept over Wenna. He was surrounded by women who deceived him. How could he not realize what had been going on? Was it her duty to tell him? She didn't know.

She turned quickly to lead her grandmother out of the room. Once they were back in the sunny bedchamber, Lady Catherine locked the door on her illicit treasures and was about to drop the key back down the neck of her gown when Wenna stepped forward, her hand out. 'I think I should have the key, Grandmother.'

The old lady frowned, but she reached up behind her neck to unclip the key chain, and then she handed it over. 'What happens now, Rowenna?'

'I'm not sure yet what I am going to do.' She looked up and met her grandmother's eyes. 'Don't you feel any remorse for what you've done?'

Lady Catherine met her gaze. 'I saw no wrong in relieving greedy people of what they didn't deserve to own.'

'Could that not also be an exact description of yourself, Grandmother?'

The old lady's shoulders stiffened. 'That is not the way I saw it.'

'And now? Can you see the wrong you did now?'

From the expression on her grandmother's face she apparently could not. 'I have learned one thing, though,' Lady Catherine said, narrowing her eyes at Wenna. 'I've learned that there is more to my granddaughter than just being a wilful child.' She went on studying her. 'I've learned there is more than a little of myself in her,' she said.

* * *

Wenna suspected the best place to find Hal at this time of day would be out working in the fields. But did she even have the right to approach him? She hardly knew the man, and after her earlier rudeness he probably wouldn't even speak to her. But who else could she turn to? She was sure that Annie wouldn't know how to advise her. Her mind was full of contradictions as she took the cliff path to Gribble Farm at a brisk pace.

As she passed Penhalow, the Pentreaths' large cottage on the cliff top, she could see Hedra in the garden. They hadn't exactly been introduced the previous evening, but the woman had been kind to her. Two children were romping around the grass, their happy squeals drifting over the cliff top as she passed. Hedra put up a hand to shield her eyes from the sun and smiled when she recognized Wenna.

'Come and join us,' she called. 'The sun is warm on this side of the house.'

'I'm on my way to see Mr Pentreath . . . em, Hal,' Wenna called back. 'I need his advice about something.'

Hedra looked surprised, but it was

hardly any of her business what advice this young woman was seeking from Hal. 'Well, later then. If you have the time, then do call in and share a dish of tea with me.'

Wenna called back a thank-you, unaware of the smile that crossed Hedra's face as she watched her make her way along the cliff path towards Gribble Farm.

Hal was out working in the field with his brother Luk as Wenna approached. It wasn't exactly the right environment to share the things she wanted to discuss with him, but then what would be?

Now that she was here, she felt more nervous than ever. She wasn't at all sure she was doing the right thing. What if Hal wanted nothing more to do with her once he learned what her grandmother had been up to? The *Southern Star* had belonged to Dewi's father, after all. And she was family!

Wenna was on the point of turning tail and hurrying back along the path when Hal looked up from his digging and saw her. He paused for a moment, then lifted his arm in greeting. She returned his wave, a feeling of nausea beginning to rise inside her as she watched him make his way across the field towards her. His sleeves were rolled up and the buttons on his shirt were undone, exposing his tanned weather-beaten chest. His worried frown made her heart beat faster.

'Can I help you? Is something wrong?'

'I'm fine,' she said quickly. 'I didn't mean to interrupt your work.'

'I'm almost finished anyway. Come back to the house. Ma usually has a jug of milk and some fresh baked biscuits on the table this time of day.'

Wenna glanced nervously at Hal's younger brother, who had stopped his work and was giving her a curious stare. She shot out a hand. 'My name's Wenna,' she said. 'And I'll understand if you send me packing, but I think I might need your help.' She screwed up her eyes and squinted up at him. 'But if you don't want to speak to me, then that's fine, and I — '

'Whoa,' he said, laughing. 'Can we just go back a bit?' He took her hand and shook it. 'Pleased to meet you, Wenna. I'm Hal. Now what's all this about?'

'Actually, em . . . Hal, it would be easier if we could just walk for a bit.'

They took off up the path in the opposite direction to Penhalow. Wenna had no idea where to begin a conversation like this, so she just jumped in. 'It's about my grandmother,' she said. 'She's done something terrible.'

Over the next half-hour she told Hal about the old lady and her scandalous activities. If he was shocked he hadn't shown it, nor did he make any comment until she had finished.

They stopped by a large boulder and sat, gazing out across the sea. Wenna slid Hal a glance. His expression was stony. Was he remembering, as she was, all those poor crew members of the

*Southern Star*? They had done nothing to deserve being attacked by Boskano and his evil followers. It was all her grandmother's fault, which probably made it her fault too.

She swallowed. 'Do you hate me, Hal?' Her voice came out in a strange squeak.

Hal turned to stare at her. 'I'm still trying to take all this in. But hate you? Why would I hate you?'

'Because of my grandmother.'

'Exactly! It was your grandmother who caused these things to happen, not you.' He took her hands in his. They were still grimy from the fields, but Wenna didn't care. She had told Hal and he didn't blame her. It was what she had been fearing the most . . . but he didn't blame her.

'I don't know what to do,' she said meekly. 'That's why I've come to you.'

Hal threw his head back and let out a loud, powerful sigh. 'She is still your grandmother. I'm guessing you don't want to involve the authorities?'

Wenna shook her head. 'I can't do that, but I do want to give all the things she's acquired through her dishonest trade back to their rightful owners.'

Hal pressed his lips together. 'That could be more difficult than it sounds, especially since we have no idea who the items should be returned to.'

'I did have another thought,' Wenna said slowly, watching Hal's expression. 'My grandmother said she only stole from really rich people — people who would not even miss the things they lost. If we could not return the items to their original owners, perhaps we could use them in a different way.'

'I'm not sure I follow you.'

'Well, I was thinking . . . ' She put up her hands in a gesture of defence. 'And I'm not suggesting it would be the right thing to do, because we must still give it much consideration. But I was thinking, what if we distribute the proceeds from the sale of some of these things to the poor communities in Cornwall?'

Hal's expression gave nothing away, but there was a new light in his eyes.

'Well?' Wenna urged. 'Would that be something worth considering?'

'Hmm,' Hal said. 'Could be. We have to discuss it with Jem and Hedra though . . . and Kit and Dewi.'

'Dewi?' Wenna repeated in alarm. She knew from the snatches of conversation she had overheard the previous night that the *Southern Star* was owned by Dewi St Neot's father. 'Do we have to tell Dewi? After what my grandmother did to her father, she won't even want to speak to me.'

'She'll like that you are offering a way for her father to be recompensed for the loss of his ship.'

Wenna hadn't thought of that. It would be wonderful if they could use some of the proceeds from the sale of what her grandmother described as her treasures to pay back those who deserved to be helped.

'Could we really do that?'

Hal nodded. 'But first we must

discuss it with the others. After that, I suppose it depends on the value of your grandmother's ill-gotten gains.'

# 9

Dewi had been watching the moor road for the first sight of her father's horse since dawn.

'He'll be here.' Kit laughed, coming to take his wife in his arms. 'And all the sooner if you stop searching that road for him.'

Dewi sighed. 'I'm just concerned for him. The loss of the *Southern Star* will have taken its toll. His mood could be very low now for all I know.'

'Your father is stronger than you give him credit for, my love. And he has Sarah by his side.'

'I know; you're right. But it doesn't stop me worrying. I still can't quite believe what happened. All those poor men.'

'Fortunately all the crew members who were injured are recovering well — and they have you to thank for that.'

'More than just me, Kit. Hedra was magnificent, as were all the women from the cove.' The memory of their friends coming together to offer what help they could brought a lump to her throat.

'How is Captain Colby this morning?' Kit asked. 'Have you looked in on him yet?'

Dewi nodded. 'I think he is feeling a little apprehensive about my father's arrival. It's ridiculous, but I believe he blames himself for that pirate attack.'

'That's nonsense,' Kit said. 'Your father would never hold him responsible.'

'Of course he wouldn't, but I can understand how the captain feels. The *Southern Star*, and the safety of all those on board, was his responsibility. It cannot be easy losing a ship.'

It was mid-afternoon when the two riders cantered into sight. Richard Luscombe rode out ahead of his companion, his chestnut mare holding its head high.

'They're here!' Dewi called excitedly from the window of the bedchamber that gave the best view of the winding track across the moor. She flew down the wide stone staircase and out the great front door. Her father saw her and lifted an arm in greeting. Dewi waved back. Kit appeared as the riders came into the yard. He stepped forward to help his father-in-law dismount.

Dewi rushed headlong into his arms. 'I've been watching for you,' she said breathlessly, standing on tiptoe to brush the dust of the long ride from her father's shoulder. 'How is Sarah?'

'We are both well.' He held his daughter at arm's length. 'And you, Dewi? How are you?'

'All the better for seeing you, Father.' She laughed. 'I've been watching for you.'

'Only since dawn.' Kit grinned. 'I have never seen your daughter so excited, Richard.' He turned to shake hands with Aaron Scobie. 'We miss you down at the boatyard, Aaron.' He sent a teasing glance in Richard's direction. 'Is my father-in-law treating you well at Luscombe Shipping?'

'He always did, Kit.' Aaron grinned back. 'But as you know, it suited Lucy to be back in Plymouth, so . . . ' His shoulders rose in an amiable shrug that said whatever his young wife wanted she got.

Dewi had been waiting her turn to hug Aaron. She held out her arms. 'It's good to see you again. How is Lucy?'

'She's blooming,' Aaron said. The glint of pride in his eye was unmistakable. 'She asked to be remembered to you.'

Dewi's mind went instantly to the pretty blonde-haired woman who had once been her maid, but was now her best friend. The two of them had come through many adventures together, including being shipwrecked when they stowed away on another of her father's ships.

The *Lady Emma* had been lured onto the rocks off Mellin Cove by a band of wreckers. Dewi had been rescued by Kit, but they had to search long and hard for Lucy before Dewi discovered her many days later up on the moors in the wreckers' camp.

'How long does Lucy have to go now?' she asked.

'Three weeks,' Aaron said, his eyes still shining. 'We can hardly wait.'

Dewi tried to picture her friends as parents. It wasn't difficult. She was in no doubt that they would make wonderful parents. 'I wish I could be there when the child arrives,' she said. 'You must both be so excited.'

'That we are, Dewi.'

'We're all excited,' Richard said. 'Your stepmother has been fashioning little bonnets for the child.'

Dewi smiled, but the sudden sadness in her heart felt like a leaden weight. Sarah should be making bonnets for *her* child. She glanced away, unaware of Kit's concerned look.

Captain Colby appeared as they walked into the Hall. Richard held out his hand and took hold of the man's shoulder. Dewi saw a tear sparkle in the captain's eyes and knew this was not an easy meeting for him. Her father recognized the man's distress too and patted his shoulder. 'We'll talk later, William. For now it is just good to see you — and looking so fit. Dewi tells me you were badly wounded.'

Captain Colby touched the bandage on his head. 'It's nothing; just a scratch.'

'It was a bit more than just a scratch, Father. Captain Colby's injuries were serious, but he still cared more about the condition of his crew than for himself.'

'Are many of the casualties still here at Mellin Hall?' Richard asked as Kit led them into the drawing room.

'Captain Colby here is the last, and he has only stayed on to greet you. All the others are on their way back to Plymouth now.'

Jesemy appeared at Dewi's side. 'I have the tea all ready, Miss Dewi. Just tell me when your visitors will be wanting it.'

Dewi glanced across the room. Kit was already at the decanter and filling glasses. 'Give them a few minutes, Jesemy, and then bring in the tray. I'm sure your lovely biscuits will be most welcome.'

Jesemy looked back at the visitors and wondered how long it had been since the two gentlemen had a good square meal. A large joint of beef was already turning on the spit over the big black kitchen range. They would enjoy that.

No mention was made of the pirate attack until after they had eaten that evening and had praised a flustered, embarrassed Jesemy for her wonderful dinner. Dewi had been about to leave the four men to their brandy when her father asked her to stay. She sat down again as Richard turned to Captain Colby.

'So, William, do you feel up to telling us what happened?'

They all sat with growing anger as the sea captain described how his ship was attacked.

'They came from nowhere,' he said. 'It was foggy in the Channel, and they took full advantage of that. We only realized we were about to come under attack when their ship drew alongside. They climbed aboard, screaming like devils and brandishing cutlasses.' A shiver ran through him. 'We had no defence other than our fists. They just cut us down without mercy.'

Dewi saw the man's hand tremble as he relived the horror. He was clearly still in shock. She was about to go to him when Kit put a hand on her arm and shook his head. 'Let him finish,' he said quietly.

She glanced at her father, who had hung his head, shaking it.

'One of them must have gone below,' Captain Colby said, 'because before we knew it they were leaping across the deck, arms full of casks and boxes from the hold.' He swallowed. 'But even then they had not finished. I don't know where the torches came from, but suddenly the sails were blazing, and fire was streaking across the deck.'

The man cleared his throat and looked away, but not before Dewi saw the muscles in his neck flex in anger. 'That's when the fishing fleet from here at Mellin Cove appeared. The pirates were already retreating. I can still hear their whoops of laughter. They had no care for the men they had mercilessly tried to cut to pieces.' He broke off, looking across at Richard Luscombe. 'I lost your ship, sir.' His voice was shaking. 'It was my fault that the *Southern Star* was put to the torch.'

Richard got up and began to pace the room. 'Whatever else this may have been, it was not your fault, William.' He spun round to stare at the man. 'You must stop blaming yourself. No one holds you responsible. I am just so sorry for the ordeal that you and your crew have been subjected to.'

'Father's right, Captain Colby,' Dewi

said. 'The loss of the *Southern Star* was a terrible thing, but the fault lies with the evil people who attacked you.'

'Do we know anything about them?' Aaron Scobie asked.

'Their ship had the name of the *Blessed Huntress*. One of my crewmen saw it.'

'Well, that's a clue, is it not?' Dewi asked.

'Probably not,' Aaron said. 'They will have a new name painted across the bow by now.'

'Depends how arrogant they are,' Kit said thoughtfully. 'They may believe they are invincible.'

'So there's still a chance we may find them,' Dewi said.

'But will we find them with the goods they stole from the *Southern Star*?' her father said.

Captain Colby pushed away his still full brandy glass. 'If I can be of any help in finding these people, then of course I will.'

Richard smiled. 'I have no doubt of

that, my friend. You have told us everything you could recall about the attack.' He paused. 'And I know that cannot have been easy for you. The best thing you can do now is to return to your family. They will be anxious, and it's time you put their minds at rest.'

* * *

Captain Colby rode off with Tomas at first light next morning to catch the coach from Penzance. Dewi later saw Jesemy cross the courtyard to the stables when her husband returned with both horses. She tried to smile but her bottom lip trembled. Jesemy and Tomas were such a loving couple. The fact that they were childless never seemed to affect that. She must learn from them. Being envious of her friends' children was wrong. They deserved to have their babies. She was happy for them.

Kit and her father had gone down to

the boatyard in Dizzard Cove immediately after breakfast. Aaron lingered behind to wait for Dewi. 'Father puts on a good show of coping with all this, but I know the loss of the *Southern Star* has really affected him,' she said as they walked.

'Richard is tougher than you think. This idea of Kit's to build a new ship has really engaged him.'

'Kit started on the design soon after we learned what had happened. We could never build such a vessel ourselves — the boatyard does not have the capacity for that — but the designs should help Father to do so.'

'My thoughts exactly. The *Southern Star* was an old lady in need of many repairs. Don't get me wrong; she was seaworthy enough. I have inspected her myself. But there was not a great deal more life left in her, not without some serious investment in her structure. So you see, Dewi, Richard is not as distressed about the loss of his ship as you might imagine.'

'Really?' Dewi couldn't hide the surprise in her voice. She was already feeling a wave of relief wash over her.

'What upsets and angers your father about this is the loss of the precious goods he had hidden in his cabin,' Aaron said. 'He would dearly love to recover them.'

* * *

Richard and Aaron had already set off back to Plymouth when Hal and Wenna turned up at Mellin Hall. The appearance of the pair had Kit and Dewi exchanging a look. They had immediately recognized the young woman from her presence when the injured seamen had been brought to the Hall, but what was she doing here now with Hal?

Dewi ushered them into the drawing room as Kit poured the drinks. 'Wenna has something to tell you both,' Hal said, accepting the offered glass of Madeira, 'and the sooner you hear this the better.'

'This all sounds very mysterious,' Dewi said, smiling, as she and Kit settled themselves to hear Wenna's story. Their eyes widened in growing astonishment as she spoke.

'That's about the size of it,' Hal said when Wenna had finished.

Dewi sank deeper into her chair and looked from one to the other. 'You're telling us that your grandmother is responsible for the attack on my father's ship . . . for all those poor sailors almost dying?'

'I knew you would blame me,' Wenna said miserably. 'I'm so very sorry, but I had to tell you.'

'You should both thank her,' Hal said, turning to Wenna. 'I think you were very brave telling us your secret.'

'And so do I,' Kit said.

They all looked at Dewi, who had turned very pale. Kit crossed the room and stroked his wife's cheek. 'Are you all right, my love?'

Dewi nodded. 'It's a lot to take in.' She turned to Wenna. 'Thank you for coming here to tell us. It can't have been easy.'

'There's more,' Hal said. 'Tell them the rest, Wenna.'

Wenna took a deep breath. Outlining their plan had not been as difficult as she had imagined, but it didn't seem to be being met with approval.

'I'm not sure that's even legal,' Kit said.

'Smuggling is not legal,' Hal reminded him. 'But there isn't a family in the cove that's not involved in it.'

'This is different,' Kit protested. 'We would be profiting from the work of pirates.'

'Think of it as a redistribution of wealth,' Hal said. 'As a restoration of justice . . . our kind of justice.'

But Kit was still unsure. Dewi had made a miraculous recovery from her earlier shock. She bounced out of her chair and ran across the room to throw her arms around Wenna. 'I think it is a wonderful idea,' she said breathlessly. 'Positively ingenious.'

Kit smiled. 'I daresay Richard would not be opposed to collecting the cost of building a new ship.'

'And the fishing families down in the cove wouldn't mind having a few extra coppers spend,' Hal said.

'We should wait to hear what Jem and Hedra have to say before we get too excited,' Wenna cautioned.

'Of course,' said Dewi. 'But something tells me they will have the same views as us.'

The fishing fleet was on its way back to harbour as Hal and Wenna later walked to Gribble Farm. They could see the red sails of the luggers as they rounded the headland and approached the harbour.

'Your family will be missing you,' Hal said. 'We'll have some supper, and then I'll take you home in the cart.'

The only person who was ever concerned if Wenna stayed out late was her father, and he was currently in London on parliamentary business. But she did not decline the offer. She could return to Mellin Cove to share their idea with Jem and Hedra in the morning.

# 10

Enor managed to slip out of the cottage before Annie could call him to help in the kiddley. A day spent mucking out the stables and doing other menial tasks at Mellin Hall was enough work for anyone. He frowned. He shouldn't be taking orders from anyone up there. It should be he who was giving the orders.

He set off away from the harbour, up the path, and struck out across the cliffs. He had thinking to do. The moon was casting a silvery path on the ocean, but he did not notice that. In his mind he was back on the pathetically meagre plot of land his parents described as a farm. Why would they be satisfied with that when there was so much more available to them? He had no intention of being so humble.

He hadn't had the whole story, not all at once. Bits of it came to him over the years; snatches of conversations between his parents. Only when he patched them all together did they make sense. He could remember his excitement when he realized the full potential of what had happened in the past.

Penhalow Cottage was just ahead in an elevated position on the left. He slowed his step as he passed it. The Pentreaths would be sitting inside now. He tried to imagine them at the dining table, a village girl waiting on them and bringing them their food.

In the distance he could see the outline of Gribble Farm. Jem Pentreath would have been working the land now if he hadn't got ideas above his station. Ploughing the fields was not good enough for him; he had to have his fishing boat. Now he had two of them, and another was being built in the St Neots' yard.

He stopped, gazing out to sea, wondering if the boatyard at Dizzard Cove would also be part of his inheritance. A smile spread across his face. What a fine shock that would be for the St Neots. Not only would Kit lose the Hall and all of Mellin Cove, but he would also lose his yard. Enor's smile grew broader. Now that was a very satisfying thought.

Smoke curled from the chimneys of Penhalow. It conjured up another picture of an elegant parlour, a blazing fire, and two people who had a very comfortable life. Pentreath had done all right for himself. He had known what he was doing when he married into the St Neots. Enor wondered if Jem's wife Hedra ever felt that she had married beneath her. He'd watched in the churchyard as she fussed over her mother-in-law, Sally Pentreath. He wasn't sure why that had irritated him, but it had. No one had ever fussed over him.

The moon slipped behind a cloud, and the cliff top was suddenly plunged into darkness. A breeze had got up and he shivered, thrusting his hands deep into the pockets of his breeches as he hunched his shoulders and headed out over the rough moors.

By the time he returned to the Rosens' cottage, he knew exactly what he had to do.

* * *

When Enor arrived at the Hall the next morning and walked into the kitchen, Tomas was seated at the table shoveling the remains of an enormous fried breakfast into his mouth as Jesemy stirred a pot on the stove. The sound of clattering dishes took Enor's eye to the sink in the far corner as the kitchen maid, Ellen Manky, washed the plates. He thought they took advantage of the girl, given how simple she was. But it was none of his business and he said nothing.

Jesemy turned as he entered. ''Ave you eaten, lad?'

Enor nodded. His had been a more meagre meal than the one Tomas was now consuming: a chunk of bread and some milk. He had turned down Annie's offer of an egg. He wasn't greedy.

'I'll make a start, shall I, Tomas?' he said, nodding towards the stables.

'Aye, an' I'll be right behind you.' The mumbled words came through a mouthful of food.

Enor turned, saving his sneer for when he crossed the yard. He should have been nervous given what he had to do that day, but he wasn't. He knew exactly how he would do this. He needed to get St Neot on his own, and the best time to do that was on his morning ride. Well, this morning Master Kit would have a companion.

Enor didn't lift his head when Tomas came into the stable. 'Master'll be here any moment. Is Sabre ready for him?'

'He is,' Enor answered, hiding his smile. He had saddled up another horse and would be off at St Neot's heels as soon as he galloped away.

* * *

Kit had reached Satan's Folly before Enor caught up with him. He slowed, reining in his horse as the other rider approached.

'Enor!' Alarm flashed across Kit's face. He twisted round in the saddle to face him. 'Has something happened at Mellin Hall?'

A smile twisted Enor's lips. 'Not the way you mean. But something is definitely about to happen.'

Kit's black stallion pawed the ground, impatient to be off on his gallop. He steadied his mount, frowning. 'You are speaking in riddles, man. Explain yourself. Either something has happened at the Hall or it hasn't.'

'This is what we need to talk about.' Enor was smirking. 'Shall we dismount?'

The younger man's arrogance was beginning to irritate Kit. 'We will do no such thing until you state your business.'

Dismounting now, while St Neot remained in the saddle, would put Enor at a definite disadvantage; and besides, it wasn't necessary. He could deliver what he wanted to say from where he was. 'I have a story to relate . . . one you would do well to heed, Mr St Neot.' He paused, looking up at the stone edifice that was Satan's Folly — one of many such ancient relics that littered the moors. Several years earlier, Satan's Folly had been used as a hiding place by a murderous band of smugglers and wreckers who had launched an audacious attack on Kit's shipyard at Dizzard Cove, attempting to steal the ship he was building for two rich brothers from Plymouth.

Enor took a quick breath and faced the other rider. 'The thing is, Kit . . . You don't mind my calling you Kit?'

Kit frowned at him.

The man smiled. 'It's about Mellin Hall — and a small matter of ownership.'

Kit's eyes were thunderous. 'What

nonsense is this? Have you lost your mind?'

Enor Vingoe's smile broadened. There was menace in his voice as he said, 'Mellin Hall belongs to me. You had no right to claim that inheritance.'

Kit stared at him. 'Are you ill?'

'I am perfectly well, thank you, and what I tell you is true.' Enor continued to smile. 'Are you sure you don't want to dismount? This story could take some time in the telling.'

'I have no intention of listening to you.' Kit tugged on his reins and the horse wheeled round, and Enor reached across and grabbed the reins. But Kit was too quick for him. He leapt from his horse and made a grab for Enor, yanking him down and throwing him to the ground. He landed unceremoniously in a bush and let out a yell as the gorse pricked through his breeches.

Kit immediately regretted his actions, but the man had kindled his fury. His arrogance was unbelievable. He watched him struggle to his feet, rubbing his rear end.

'You can get as violent as you like,' Enor hissed, 'but it still does not change the facts. Mellin Hall — in fact, the entire estate — belongs to me.'

Kit folded his arms and fixed the man with a hard stare. 'Tell your preposterous story,' he said. 'I'm listening.'

'It goes back a few years to the time my grandmother, Mary Vingoe, worked as a maid at the Hall.'

'Go on,' Kit growled.

'It was in the days of Sir Edward Constantine and his wife, Cordelia. He was nice . . . kind to Mary, or so she thought. He filled her head with ideas above her station. He was going to get rid of Cordelia and marry her.' He paused, glancing at Kit's face and taking pleasure at his obvious growing anger. 'It was as I said. Mary was a simple young woman and it had been easy for Edward to turn her head. Before she knew what was happening, she was with child. Edward was the father.' He paused again, letting this revelation sink in before adding, 'Mary's son . . . My father, Peder, was Sir Edward's first child.' He smiled. 'And as everyone knows, the eldest child is the one who inherits.'

'That is preposterous. Your story is outrageous. You have made the whole thing up.'

'You know that is not true,' Enor sneered. 'My father is old Sir Edward's son. His daughter Morwenna had no right to the inheritance that fell to her. Your uncle . . . ' He frowned as though trying to remember the man's name. Thomas, wasn't it? 'Yes, that was it — Thomas. He died soon after your aunt Morwenna passed away. But you see, Kit, Thomas had no right to leave Mellin Hall to you. It was never his to leave.'

'If what you say is true — and I know that it is not — then why has your father never tried to claim what you say was his inheritance?'

A flush of annoyance infused Enor's

face. 'My father is a weak, simple man. He lacks my courage. I will fight for what is rightly mine. He will not.'

'So your father still lives?'

Enor saw where this was going and jumped to his own defence. 'My father has reneged on his right to inherit. It is up to me to assert my claim now.'

Kit turned, and in one smooth, swift movement leapt back on his horse. The animal's head went up in response. At last he was to have that gallop across the moors. Kit looked down on Enor and raised an eyebrow. 'Submit your documents of proof to my notary in Penzance. You do have such documents, I take it?'

The look of concern on the younger man's face supplied the satisfaction Kit needed. There was no proof, and there were no such documents. He looked down on him. 'Return that horse you are riding back to my stable — and then leave. I don't expect to see you again.'

Enor Vingoe was left staring after

horse and rider as they took off in a cloud of dust. His eyes narrowed to vengeful slits.

Kit rode his horse hard, going further than his usual morning ride. The man had outraged him. He hardly dared to think it, but what if there had been a grain of truth in what he'd said? Vingoe had no proof to back up his claim, but could Kit verify his right to inherit Mellin Hall?

He slowed Sabre to a trot, bringing the stallion to a halt. He was closer to the cliff edge than he'd realized. He stayed mounted, stroking Sabre's neck. It was glistening with sweat. 'Sorry, old boy,' he said. 'I shouldn't have taken my mood out on you.'

The horse gave a gentle neigh, throwing its head back as though in response. The two had been together since Kit was a boy at Penmere. The thought took him back to the day he learned of his inheritance. The family had been plunged into gloom since the news of his Uncle Thomas's death at

Mellin Hall, only a few short months after his beloved Morwenna. But further shock lay ahead when Kit had accompanied his father Matthew and older brother Nathan to the notary's office in Penzance for the reading of Thomas's will.

His uncle Edgar, an unrepentant rogue who had moved uninvited into the Hall with Thomas and Morwenna, had believed Mellin Hall would come to him. Kit still remembered the man's fury when he learned the truth. He'd thundered out of the notary's, threatening revenge on the entire St Neot family.

The ride back to Penmere Manor had seemed unreal that day. With Thomas and Morwenna childless, Kit had assumed that his father would have inherited Mellin Hall and the cove. The last thing he'd been expecting was for his uncle to leave everything to him. But he had, and his family had applauded the decision. Kit had persuaded his sister Hedra to accompany him and help him run his new inheritance.

Edgar had stayed on at the Hall after Thomas's death, but in the months before, as his brother's health slid into decline, Edgar had succeeded in stripping the place of its best furniture. He sacked the servants and increased the rents of the tenants in the cottages at the harbour. The whole of Mellin Cove lived in terror of him.

At first the people had also distrusted Kit and Hedra, believing the brother and sister would run the estate with the same neglect and cruelty as their uncle, Edgar St Neot. But when they learned that Kit had ordered Edgar out of the Hall and told him to stay out of Mellin Cove, they dared to hope that their fortunes might change.

Kit's head was full of memories. He dismounted, stroking his horse's mane as it grazed on the grass. He looked out along the coast, taking comfort from the familiar stretch of cliffs. Beyond the headland lay the road to Penmere. Nathan farmed the land now, and his wife Rachel ran the household. The longing to see them all again was overwhelming. Suddenly he knew what to do. He would ride to Penmere Manor with Dewi. The St Neots needed to call a family conference.

Tomas Sweet had been watching for his master's return, and came out to meet Kit as his horse clip-clopped across the cobbled courtyard. He held the reins, keeping the horse steady as Kit dismounted. 'I thought something must have happened, Master Kit,' he said anxiously. 'Young Vingoe rode in here like all the devils in hell were after him. He leapt down from the horse and just took off.'

'Then let's hope that is the last we see of him,' Kit said grimly.

Tomas was still staring after him, his brow creased in confusion, as Kit strode across the yard and into the Hall. Dewi was nowhere to be seen, so Kit went in search of Jesemy. He found her in the kitchen. 'I'm looking for Dewi,' he said.

'She's gone down Dizzard Cove, sir.'

Of course — why hadn't he thought of that? She was working with him on the design of Jem's new fishing boat. It was all but finished, but there were a few minor tweaks to be made, and he knew his wife wouldn't be satisfied until the boat was as perfect as it possibly could be.

About a hundred yards from the Hall, the path forked. One route wound down to the cove, while the other carried on along the cliff path, with another fork that led to Dizzard Cove and Kit's small boatbuilding yard. He glanced down at the harbour as he passed. With the fishing fleet at sea, it all looked very peaceful. Some of the women were sitting outside their cottages mending nets. Life was going on at its usual pace.

Dewi was studying a design chart when Kit walked into the tiny office that overlooked the busy yard. She looked up and smiled. 'You've done a good job with Jem's boat. He will be pleased. By my reckoning, a week or so should do it.'

Kit went to stand behind her, his hands on her shoulders, his cheek resting on the top of her head. The yard provided work for many local men, and had even attracted a few more to bring their families and settle in the cove. Three new cottages had been built above the harbour, and others were being planned.

'Mellin Cove is beginning to prosper,' Dewi said, smiling, as though she had read his mind. 'And it's all thanks to you.'

Kit kissed the top of her head. 'I suspect you might have had something to do with that too, my love. There would be no yard if you hadn't encouraged me to follow my dream.' A dream that could now be in jeopardy, he thought. 'There is something I must discuss with you. Can we go back to the Hall?'

Dewi gave him a troubled stare. 'I don't like the sound of this, Kit. Tell me you're not ill.'

'No.' He laughed, helping her down from the high architect's chair. 'It's nothing like that, but a serious matter has arisen and we need to talk.'

They walked up the path, an arm around each other's waist. Dewi was desperate to know what the serious matter was, but she knew Kit would not discuss it until they had reached the privacy of the Hall. If Kit was not ill, then it must be a member of his family. Her heart lurched. What if it was *her* family? Was her father ill? Was this the serious news she was about to be told?

Dewi's heart was pounding by the time they reached Mellin Hall. Kit led her into his small study. 'Well, tell me!' she cried, as soon as he had closed the door behind them. 'Has something happened to my father? Is he ill?'

Kit gave a surprised frown. 'This has nothing to do with your father, Dewi.

It's about Mellin Hall . . . and perhaps our future.'

Dewi sank slowly into a chair, her eyes growing wide with disbelief as Kit told his story. 'But that is outrageous,' she said when he was finished. 'Surely you are not taking this man's claims seriously?'

Kit went to pour himself a glass of Madeira wine from a decanter on the silver tray by his desk. He waved a glass at Dewi, inviting her to join him. She shook her head. He took a sip of the wine and gave a resigned sigh. 'The claim has to be investigated.'

'But how? Where does one start to investigate something like this?'

'With my family. We must go to Penmere Manor, Dewi.'

# 11

The three riders kept up a steady pace across the moor. 'Was Hedra very upset to stay at home with the children?' Kit asked Jem.

His brother-in-law gave a grim smile. 'That would be putting it mildly. Your sister is very spirited. I'm not sure she's speaking to me even now, but it would have been out of the question for her to accompany us so soon after the babies.'

Dewi had pulled out ahead of them and the men hung back, talking. 'I suppose there couldn't be any truth in what this Vingoe claims?' Jem said.

Kit frowned into the wind. 'I didn't know Sir Edward Constantine, but I have heard nothing but good of him. The man this scoundrel described is not the one I recognize.'

'How will your father take the news that your right to own Mellin Hall and the estate is being called into question?'

'He won't be happy about it. Neither will Nathan and Rachel when they hear.' He slid Jem a glance. 'You saw how Hedra reacted when I shared it with her.'

Jem nodded. 'I had to physically restrain her from riding down to the cove and knocking on the Rosens' door demanding to speak to Vingoe.'

'That wouldn't have been a good plan,' Kit said. 'It would have been all over Mellin Cove if she had done that, and just for the moment I feel this business is better kept in the family.'

'Vingoe may not share that opinion,' Jem warned. 'He could be spreading his lies all over Cornwall by now.'

'Well, let's hope that is not happening. It's difficult enough coping with his allegations without having to deal with malicious gossip.'

The men fell silent and Kit rode ahead, catching up with Dewi. 'We can stop and rest awhile if you are tiring, my love.'

'I don't want to stop. I just want to get to Penmere as soon as possible. How much longer do you think it will take us?'

They had ridden inland to cut off the extra miles the coastal track took around the headland. They would soon see the village up ahead, and the rows of miners' cottages.

'Penmere is only a short way ahead now,' Kit said.

'The family will be surprised to see us,' Dewi commented, the wind snatching at her words as she spoke them. 'We don't exactly bring good news.'

'It will be fine,' Kit said. 'Families should be together at times like these. We will take strength from each other. Father will know what to advise.'

Jem trotted his horse forward to come alongside them. He pointed ahead. 'Isn't that the village?'

'It is.' Kit looked at Dewi. 'We are almost home.'

The first sight of his childhood home, outlined against the far ocean and sky, made Kit's heart leap. The chimneys were smoking, and images of the people inside the old manor house flitted through his mind. It was late afternoon and his father would be in his study, a favourite pipe in his mouth as he read. Nathan would have come in from the fields.

He smiled at the thought of the children, four-year-old Conan and eleven-year-old Loveday, running excitedly to greet him. Rachel would be checking that all was well in the kitchen. At this time of day he knew their cook, Bessie Bunt, would have the family's evening meal well under way. Bessie and her husband Jonas had been at Penmere Manor for so long that they were regarded more as members of the family than servants. They reminded him of Jesemy and Tomas at Mellin Hall. He and Dewi were lucky to have such a good and loyal couple looking after them.

* * *

It was Rachel who heard the horses first. The windows in the drawing room looked out over the cliff to the sea, but another at the side of the house gave a view of the track by which visitors approached. 'There are riders coming.' She knocked on the door of her father-in-law's study. 'I think it's Kit.'

The door flew open and Matthew came striding out, joining Rachel at the window. Dusk was falling and the riders were not yet properly in sight, but Matthew knew immediately that it was his son. 'Come, Rachel. Let's give them a welcome.'

The doors of Penmere Manor opened, flooding the forecourt with light.

'It's Father,' said Kit. 'Look, Dewi — he and Rachel have come to meet us.'

The sight of the familiar figures standing in the doorway filled Dewi with relief. She had been starting to imagine they would never reach the manor.

'My boy!' Matthew came striding

forward, unable to conceal his worried frown. 'And Dewi and Jem, too. Has something happened?'

'It's not Hedra, is it?' Rachel said, her hand going to her mouth.

'Hedra's fine,' Jem assured them, dismounting and coming forward. 'Most displeased of course that she couldn't join us, but a half day's riding so soon after the births did not strike me as a good idea. She has taken the children to Gribble Farm. Ma was delighted to have their company.'

'How is your dear mother, Jem? This must be such a difficult time for her.'

'She's coping, sir.'

Rachel hurried ahead to help Dewi from her horse as Kit dismounted. Jonas had appeared from the side of the house to attend to the horses.

'Well, let's not stand out in the cold,' Matthew said, rubbing his hands together. 'There's a blazing fire inside. Let's go in, and you can tell us what this unexpected visit is all about.'

Matthew had taken Jem and Kit into

his study as Dewi followed Rachel upstairs to Kit's old room, which had been redecorated the previous year. The masculine dark green drapes had been replaced by softer cream brocade that matched the bed canopy. Cosy chocolate-coloured rugs were scattered on the wooden floor. The furniture was the same sturdy polished mahogany, but it gave an air of solidity that was comforting to Dewi.

'I expect you will want to rest after your long ride,' Rachel said, going around the room plumping up cushions on the chairs and bed.

'I'd much rather talk,' Dewi said, sinking into the big dark armchair.

Rachel took both Dewi's hands in her own and sat opposite on the edge of the bed. 'What's this all about, Dewi? I don't think I have ever seen Kit look so worried.'

Dewi leaned back and closed her eyes.

Rachel frowned. 'Is it that bad?'

'I honestly don't know, Rachel.' She

let out a long lingering sigh. 'Kit might lose Mellin Hall.'

Rachel stared at her, eyes wide with alarm. 'But how . . . what?'

Over the next ten minutes, Dewi related the events that had rocked her and Kit's world. When she finished, Rachel was still staring at her in disbelief. 'That's it,' Dewi said. 'The whole horrible story.'

'Could there be any truth in this man's claim?' Rachel asked.

'Kit thinks not. He didn't know Sir Edward, of course, but the man had such a good reputation.' She threw up her hands. 'We just don't know. That's why we are here. We need Matthew's wisdom.'

Rachel tried not to show her shock. She was thinking of how this news would affect her husband, Nathan. The two brothers were close. She wished he hadn't gone off to Truro on farm business. He wasn't expected back at Penmere until morning. She snapped her mind back to the present. What

Dewi and Kit needed most now was support.

'Hedra wanted to come with us of course,' Dewi said quietly. 'But as Jem said, he had to put his foot down.'

'I should think so,' Rachel said.

A smile drifted across Dewi's face. 'Poor Hedra. She was so angry with Jem. She said this was family business and she should be here with the rest of us. It took quite a bit of persuading on his part to make her see the sensible thing to do was to stay behind with the children.'

'Well, I'm glad she saw sense. She has quite enough on her hands looking after four children.'

Dewi gave a wistful nod. She and Kit had been wed for two years, and although they were truly happy together, she constantly had to fight back sadness that there was no sign of any babies coming along for them. She'd got cross with herself when Hedra's time came and she surprised everyone by producing two babies. It hadn't seemed fair to Dewi when she so longed for a child. But that was mean-minded. She was pleased for Hedra and Jem, of course she was. The couple's joy was obvious. One day it would be her and Kit's turn to be parents . . . one day.

'Is Hedra well?' Rachel asked.

Dewi smiled, remembering her sister-in-law's glowing good health. 'She thrives on bearing children. She's wonderful.'

Rachel reached across and squeezed her hand. 'This will all work out. We will make sure that it does.' But she couldn't stop her thoughts straying to Kit. They had all been surprised when Thomas St Neot, Kit's uncle, bequeathed Mellin Hall and the estate to him. It had been a welcome surprise, for they all knew how well Kit would shoulder that responsibility. Rachel hadn't expected Hedra to go with him, of course. They were more like sisters to each other than sisters-in-law. She'd had to force herself not to be selfish. Moving to Mellin Cove with Kit to help him run the estate had been the best decision Hedra had ever made.

That was where Hedra had met and married Jem after all, and now they had four children. Rachel had never known Hedra so happy. She would be beside herself with worry right now.

* * *

Downstairs in Matthew's study, the three men were on their second glasses of brandy. Matthew leaned back in his chair, pipe between his teeth. 'This man Vingoe sounds like an adventurer. Do you know anything about his family, Kit?'

'He has relatives in the cove, an Annie and Jory Rosen. Annie was brought up in one of the cottages down by the harbour. When she learned that it was unoccupied, she came to see me and asked if she and her husband might become my tenants.'

Matthew puffed out smoke. 'What relation is she to this Vingoe?'

'An aunt, I think. Possibly a great-aunt. I'm not exactly sure.'

'Do you think the Rosens are part of this plot?' Matthew asked. 'Could they have returned to Mellin Cove to work with the man?'

Kit shrugged. 'I don't honestly know. I wouldn't have thought so, but then I believed Enor to be a good man when Tomas hired him to work in the stables.'

Jem drained his glass and put it on Matthew's desk. 'I agree with Kit. I can't believe the Rosens have any part in this. They're good people. But Enor has been living with them, so I suppose we must consider that they knew what he was up to.'

'I don't think any of us know that, Jem,' said Kit. 'It could be that they have been deceived as much as the rest of us. When the Rosens get to hear of this, I suspect they will be as shocked and angry as we are.'

'It seems to me,' Matthew said, 'that this can't be left to what you suspect. You need to ask Mrs Rosen what she knows. She will be able to tell you about her family history.'

'I see what you're saying, sir,' Jem said. 'If Enor's story had been true, and the Vingoe family really did believe they were entitled to inherit Mellin Hall, then why have they not laid claim to it before now?'

Matthew nodded. 'That would be my thinking. You need to speak to Annie Rosen, Kit.'

The woman was the first person Kit had thought of as he took off across the moor yesterday, leaving Enor Vingoe staring after him. The trouble was, as soon as he discussed this with anyone outside the family, the greater the chance of gossip spreading. It was the last thing the poor fishing families of Mellin Cove needed to hear. He couldn't bear subjecting them to the kind of fear and insecurity they would be bound to feel once Vingoe's claim became public.

Kit tried to think back to what Annie had told him about herself at that first meeting. She had talked about being brought up in Mellin Cove. He gave an involuntary frown. That would put the Vingoe family in the village at the right time to back up Enor Vingoe's story, but that didn't make it true.

He looked up and met his father's eyes. 'Opening this subject with Annie would be the start of making it public. I'm not sure I'm ready to do that yet.'

'It might already be too late for that,' Jem said. 'For all we know, this story is already all over Mellin Cove.'

'That's true,' Kit conceded. 'But the opposite may also be the case. If Enor has not been talking about his claim, then Annie may not be aware of any of this.'

'But what if she does know?' Jem said. 'What if she is the one behind this? I know they are good people, but Enor is staying with her and Jory after all. I find it hard to believe they have not spoken about it.'

Kit shook his head. 'I saw a very different side of young Vingoe yesterday from the willing and amiable stable hand he had portrayed himself to be. I saw venom and hatred. I didn't see a man who would be told what to do.' He tipped back the remains of his brandy and narrowed his eyes at that last memory of Vingoe's sneering face. 'He's also after the boatyard,' he said quietly.

'How could he possibly have any claim on that?' Jem was outraged. 'You and Dewi built that up. There was no boatyard at Dizzard Cove before then.'

Kit sighed. 'There was, actually. Uncle Thomas was building boats down there years ago. He wasn't exactly successful at it and it all fell into disrepair, but it was part of the estate.'

'Enor Vingoe knows nothing about boats.' Jem's voice was rising. 'I doubt if he has ever even been on board a lugger.'

'His knowledge or otherwise matters little, Jem,' Kit said. 'The fact that he believes he can take the boatyard from me is enough to satisfy him. I told you, he hates me!'

Matthew had got up to stand by the window. The drapes had not yet been drawn in his study, and the lights from the north-facing rooms in the old manor house illuminated the wide track that led to Penmere village. 'Strong words to use, Kit,' he said thoughtfully. 'If this fellow honestly despises you, as you suspect, then perhaps he really does believe he has a claim on Mellin Hall.'

'You mean he's not just an opportunist trying his luck?' Jem said.

'He may well be that, Jem. He could be — and probably is — making all of this up.'

'I feel a 'but' coming,' Kit said.

Matthew's broad shoulders rose in a shrug. 'If this Vingoe feels a great injustice has been done to him; if he truly believes, however misguidedly, that you have stolen something that rightfully belongs to him — then he would be filled with the kind of hatred you describe.'

Kit sighed. 'It's a quandary knowing what to do for the best.' He turned to his father. 'What should I do, sir?'

'I wish I had all the answers for you, Kit, but I do know that Vingoe can do nothing without proof. If he insists on going ahead with this, then it will ultimately become a matter for the courts. And if you believe this Annie to be unaware of her relative's claims, and feel confident she would treat with discretion anything you share with her, then perhaps you should speak with her.' He shrugged again. 'It has to be your decision, Kit.'

* * *

Dinner that evening had been a subdued affair, with everyone avoiding the subject of Enor Vingoe. But later in their bedchamber, when Dewi climbed into the high four-poster beside Kit, she said, 'Has this visit been helpful? Has Matthew been able to advise you?'

Kit took his wife's face in his hands. 'Such a worried little look.' He smiled down at her. 'My father has been helpful, yes. He didn't tell me what to do, but he pointed the way to a few possibilities.'

Dewi swallowed. She'd been trying to imagine what life away from Mellin Cove would be like. It hadn't been a pleasant thought — and then there was the boatyard. Was that also in jeopardy? She could feel her blood rising. No! No one would take Dizzard Cove from them! She tried to imagine what her father would do under such circumstances. It didn't take much thought. He would fight — just as she and Kit would fight for everything they held dear.

'Did these possibilities you speak of involve violence?' There was an edge to Dewi's voice.

Kit frowned. 'Violence?'

She looked up and met his eyes. 'Yes . . . violence!'

* * *

Dewi's daring idea of the previous night was still tracking back and forth through Kit's mind as the three of them waved their goodbyes to the family next morning and set off on the long ride back to Mellin Hall. He'd been shocked at first by its audacity.

How could his sweet little Dewi even consider such a thing? He was remembering the slight body he had pulled from the waves more dead than alive after the ship she had been on board was lured by wreckers onto rocks at Mellin Cove. Dressed in a youth's clothing, he'd thought she was a cabin boy. And then he'd seen that glorious ebony hair tumbling about her as Jesemy fussed around her young patient, and his heart had leapt.

She was a girl from the sea with no memory of who she was or how she came to be on the doomed ship. With his help, her memory had gradually returned, only to cause her anguish for the friend she was told had perished with the ship. Only Dewi had believed her maid, Lucy Coombe, was still alive — and she'd refused to give up hope until she found her.

Remembering all this, Kit didn't know why he'd even been surprised about the plan she'd described for dealing with Enor Vingoe. They didn't share the scheme with Jem and Hedra until they were back in Mellin Cove and sipping glasses of Madeira around the fire at Penhalow.

'Kidnap?' Hedra looked askance from Dewi to Kit. 'You cannot be serious.'

Jem turned away to hide his smile.

'Perfectly serious,' Dewi said. 'He could be taken out on one of Jem's luggers and transferred to one of my father's ships out in the Channel.'

'But it's a preposterous idea,' Hedra said. 'And I urge you not to share it with anyone outside this house.'

'Enor Vingoe will take Mellin Hall from Kit if we don't do something,' Dewi protested.

'Then we must find a way of stopping him,' Hedra said. 'A way that doesn't see all of us locked up in Bodmin Jail.'

# 12

Davy Geach was doing his best to concentrate on the slab of timber he was planing down to a smooth surface. He was trying to wipe all this constant worry from his mind, but his attention constantly strayed to the window of the small cabin that Kit used as an office.

He could see him inside, his head bent over the drawings he was studying. Every so often Kit would look up and gaze out to sea. Davy recognized a troubled man when he saw one. He knew what he had to do, but would that make him disloyal to his dead brother?

He stood up, stretching, easing away the knot in his shoulders, and glanced back at Kit. He hadn't even discussed this with his wife, Rosie. Should he wait for her advice?

But at the end of the day, he was always going to tell Kit what he knew.

He had no choice. Davy laid down his planing tool. He had wrestled with his conscience long enough. If he were to have a future at the Dizzard Cove boatyard, then he had to act now.

He pushed his fingers through his greying curly hair and took a deep breath before heading off for the cabin. Kit hadn't noticed him standing in the doorway, and Davy had to give a polite cough before he had the man's attention.

He had worked at the boatyard for eighteen months. The job had been a lifesaver at the time, and Kit St Neot had been good to him. He had even offered a plot of land above the village where Davy could build a cottage for his family. They were all settled and happy here now. Loyalty to his dead brother was one thing; loyalty to his wife and family was another. He took a deep breath. He knew he was doing the right thing.

Kit looked up and gave him a tired smile. 'Davy. How can I help you?'

Davy glanced down at his feet, trying to control the involuntary tapping. 'I'm not quite sure where to start, sir.' He swallowed. This was going to be harder than he thought. 'Please don't think I'm getting above my station, but there be a few things you need to know.' He met Kit's eyes and saw the man frown.

'You have me intrigued, Davy. What is this all about?'

'It's about my brother, Jack — my late brother, Jack.'

'Yes?'

'The thing is, sir . . . ' It was all coming out in a rush, but he'd started now. 'Our Jack was Enor Vingoe's grandfather. I suppose that makes me the lad's great-uncle.'

Kit stared at him. Was he hearing right? 'I'm sorry, I'm not quite sure what you mean.'

Davy cleared his throat. 'Things get round in a place like Mellin Cove. You hear things.' Kit was still staring at him, eyes wide. Davy went on, 'I've heard the rumours, you see, and I know there be no truth in what's going round. Enor Vingoe has no more right to inherit Mellin Hall than I have.'

Kit got up from his desk and began pacing the room. When he got to the end he wheeled round to face Davy. His hand was in the air. 'Let me get this right. You are saying that your brother — your late brother — was young Vingoe's grandfather? Do you have proof of this?'

'I don't know what proof you need, sir. I can only tell you what I know. Mary Vingoe was a housemaid up at the hall. She was engaged to our Jack. She . . . well, she got herself with child. Jack's child. They were to be married anyway, but things like that were still a great scandal at the time here in the cove. Jack wanted to be married at once, but Mary had a different idea. She had worked out that if she was to claim that Sir Edward Constantine was the child's father, then he would pay her to keep that to herself.'

Kit shook his head in disbelief, but said nothing.

'It was a wicked thing to do. I was only sixteen at the time, but I can remember how upset Jack was. Mary had told him that if he didn't go along with her plan, she would have nothing more to do with him. Poor Jack had no choice but to accept.'

Davy ran the tip of his tongue over his dry lips. He wasn't enjoying this one little bit. It was obvious from Kit's expression how angry he was. He gave another swallow and continued, 'Once Mary started to show, of course the whole village knew about her condition. Most people had assumed the child was Jack's, and it was obvious to all how besotted he was with her. No one could understand why they did not marry. But Mary had other ideas. Her plan to extort money from Sir Edward had worked. He gave her money to stop her spreading unfounded rumours, but Mary was greedy. As long as she could go on extorting money from the man, she would not marry our Jack.' He frowned. 'But things went wrong at the birth. The baby was fine and healthy. Mary wasn't doing so well. She died the next day. Jack's world fell apart. He just couldn't go on living without his Mary.'

Davy glanced to the window. In his mind's eye he could see Mellin Cove that day, and the fish store at the far end of the harbour where his brother had hanged himself.

'What happened to Jack?' Kit asked quietly.

'He took his own life.'

Kit crossed the room and put his hand on Davy's shoulder. 'I am sorry. That couldn't have been easy for you to talk about.'

For a moment there was silence in the little room. The noises of hammering and sawing continued outside, and Kit was aware of heads turning and brows furrowing as the men busy on Jem's new lugger tried to work out what business Davy had with St Neot.

'There is one thing I don't understand, Davy. Why have you never told this story before?'

'There was no reason to, sir. It was a family business. Jack would never have been happy if it had been made public just how greedy and dishonest Mary had been. The Constantines were a popular family. The locals would not have appreciated what Mary had tried to do. Some may even have blamed Jack. I couldn't possibly have revealed all of that.'

Kit was shaking his head.

'Please accept my apologies,' Davy said. 'But back then I believed I was doing the right thing.'

'Your loyalty to your brother is commendable. I can completely understand why you said nothing all these years.'

'I had no reason to say anything . . . not until now.'

'Does Enor know about this?'

Davy shook his head.

A grim smile crept over Kit's face.

'Could you possibly join me for a glass of Madeira in my study this evening, Davy? I would like you to repeat what you just told me to the man himself.'

Davy swallowed. He wasn't going to enjoy it, but he knew that it was the least he could do. 'I'll be there, sir. You can depend on me. And there's someone else who needs to know what I've just told you.'

Kit raised an eyebrow. 'Someone else?'

Davy nodded. 'I should have explained things to her as soon as I realized she was here in Mellin Cove.' He looked up and met Kit's confused eyes. 'It's Annie Rosen. She's Mary's sister.'

Kit's hand went to his forehead and he shook his head. Of course — so Annie would have known this story about Sir Edward Constantine all along. He was going over all the times they had spoken together, all the times he had been in her and Jory's company. She had given no clue about the past. Had she thought that Enor's claim to Mellin Hall had been groundless? Why had she never mentioned it? Kit could think of only one reason — Annie already knew that Davy's brother was the father of her sister's child. But if that were the case, why hadn't she come forward when Enor was spreading his story to anyone who would listen? Why hadn't she put him right?

'It's a bad business, sir. I feel responsible for what's happened.' Davy bit his lip. 'I wouldn't be surprised if you sent me packing.'

'Why would I do that? I have much to thank you for, but this has to be done properly. I'll be inviting Annie and Jory to join us at the Hall. It's time this business was aired in a proper way.'

* * *

Dewi was arranging the roses she had just cut from the garden when Kit came into the room. She saw the change in him immediately. 'Something's happened,' she said, her eyes shining. 'You have a spring in your step. Is it good news?'

'You could say that.' He smiled, crossing the room in three strides and sweeping her into his arms. 'We will be having visitors.'

'Is that the good news?' She laughed.

'Davy Geach will be coming, and I have sent word to Annie and Jory Rosen to be here. And Enor Vingoe, of course. Especially Enor Vingoe.'

Dewi narrowed her eyes and tilted her head at him. 'You're up to something. What's going on?'

Over the next ten minutes, Kit recounted what Davy had told him and watched Dewi's eyes grow wider.

'So Enor really has been lying all along?' She was shocked.

'Perhaps not. It's possible he had no knowledge of this.'

'But Annie . . . the woman's own sister. She must have known, and still she said nothing. She was prepared to

see you hounded out of Mellin Hall.'
Dewi felt a shiver run up her back. 'How could she do that when you have been so kind to them?'

'Let's not be hasty. We must wait until this evening to hear what they all have to say.'

'I think Jem and Hedra should be here. They have been as worried as us about the possibility of losing the Hall.'

'I'll send word to them,' Kit agreed. He was about to go in search of Tomas when the door flew open. Enor Vingoe stood there, an arrogant glint in his eye. He gave Kit a sneering look and strode into the room.

'I did not invite you to enter,' Kit said, the muscles in his jaw working. 'How dare you burst into our home unannounced?'

Enor spread his coat-tails and sat down in Kit's chair. His mouth curved into a cold smile. 'I think you will find that this is my home.' He glanced around the room. 'I see no signs of any preparations to vacate it.'

Dewi gasped, her fingers going to her throat.

Kit put out his hand to calm her before advancing on Enor. 'Leave my home immediately,' he ordered, his voice rising as he grabbed the man's sleeve and jerked him to his feet.

Enor was no match for Kit's height or strength, but it did not stop him protesting as he was marched unceremoniously from the room, through the hall and out the main entrance.

'This is my property, St Neot,' Enor spluttered. 'You can't evict me from my own property. I demand to be heard.'

'And you shall,' Kit said, giving Enor an extra shove that had him sprawling onto the gravel drive. 'Be back here at seven p.m. and we will get this business sorted once and for all.' He didn't wait for a response, but turned on his heel and went back into the Hall, slamming the great studded oak door behind him.

* * *

There had been no time to explain the sudden invitation to Mellin Hall to Jem and Hedra before the Rosens arrived, so each of the four faces wore expressions of curiosity. Jem looked from Kit to Dewi. 'Is someone going to tell us what this is all about?'

Annie sat beside her husband, fidgeting nervously with her ring. Enor had caused so much trouble for this family that they were bound to want them out of the village. There was a knock on the door and Tomas entered, announcing the arrival of Davy Geach. He came into the room wringing his hands and looking nervously around him.

It was another ten minutes before Enor Vingoe turned up. Dewi heaved a shaky sigh. She'd almost run out of nervous small talk. Vingoe wasn't looking quite as confident as before. Annie threw her great nephew a disgusted look. So she had been right: this was about his outrageous claim for inheritance. He had no right to behave as he had. The St Neots had been good to them, and she and Jory had been good to Enor. Now he was throwing that kindness back at them. She faced him. 'I'm ashamed you are still in this village after all the trouble you have caused.'

Jory put a hand on her arm. 'It's all right, Annie. Don't waste your breath on him. He's not worth it.'

'I only want what's mine,' Enor spat back at them.

'But it's not yours, Vingoe, is it?' Davy Geach cut in.

Hedra frowned at Jem, who shrugged his shoulders.

'Mellin Hall has never been yours to inherit,' Davy continued. 'I am ashamed that we share the same family blood. Jack would be ashamed of you an' all.'

'Jack? Who's Jack?' Vingoe hissed.

'Jack is your grandfather . . . your real grandfather. You don't have an ounce of Constantine blood in your body. And I am ashamed to admit that you are a Geach.'

Annie was on her feet, staring at Davy. She was only six years old when Enor's father Peder was born, but Mary had always claimed that he was Sir Edward's son. It hadn't made sense even back then. She could still remember the smiling fair-haired young man who spent so much time at their cottage. There had been talk of a wedding and of her being a flower girl. It was all falling into place now.

She was staring at Davy. 'Jack was your brother? But you must have known I was a Vingoe . . . that I was Mary's sister. Why did you never tell me this?'

Davy stood, nervously twirling his cap in his hands. 'It was remiss of me; I know that now. I have no excuses, except that I was protecting Jack. It seemed to me that it would serve no good purpose to have this sad business dragged up again. My brother deserved to be remembered with dignity.'

Annie rolled her eyes to the ceiling. She remembered it all now. Jack had hanged himself. Mary had broken his heart because she wouldn't marry him. Her child was Jack's, but she thought she could get money from Sir Edward if she said the boy was his.

She sank back onto her chair and Jory put an arm around her shoulders. 'I remember the row that night at the cottage when our mother begged Mary to tell the truth and marry Jack, but she wouldn't,' she said.

'You're lying. It's all lies. You're all in this together.' Enor's eyes were wild with rage. 'This is a plot to rob me of my inheritance!' he screamed at them. 'Well you won't get away with it! Mellin Hall is mine!' He poked a thumb at his chest. 'It's mine, and I'll prove it!'

'Be quiet, Enor — you're showing us all up!' Jory shouted. It was the first time Annie had ever heard him raise his voice in anger.

'This has nothing to do with you!' Enor yelled back.

Kit stepped forward. 'I think you've said enough, Vingoe. It would be best if you were to leave now.'

Jem sprang to his feet, ready to help his brother-in-law deal with the enraged man. But Kit put up a hand, stopping him from grabbing Enor. The man threw a furious glare in Annie's direction as he stormed out of the house, slamming the door.

The angry scene had stunned the room into silence, and then Kit gave a little cough. 'I apologize for that, ladies and gentlemen. I had no idea the man would behave in such a way.'

'It's me that should be apologizing, sir,' Annie said. 'He is my great-nephew, after all. His father and mother will be so upset when I tell them of this.'

'We will make sure Enor leaves Mellin Cove by morning,' Jory assured them.

'And Jory and me will be gone soon after,' Annie said.

'But why?' Dewi was out of her chair. 'This is no fault of yours, Annie — or yours, either, Jory.'

'Dewi is right,' Hedra said. 'You

cannot be held responsible for Enor's behaviour, even if he is a member of your family.' She looked across at her brother. 'Tell them, Kit. None of this is their fault.'

Kit came across and took Annie's hand, giving Jory a nod. 'Of course it's not your fault. Please don't leave Mellin Cove.' He smiled. 'We need you here.'

All eyes were on Annie as she wiped away a tear. Jory was not exactly looking dry-eyed either. 'We'll be staying,' he said. 'Thank you.'

# 13

Enor hadn't returned to the Rosens' cottage that night. He'd spent the hours of darkness tramping the moors, punching the air and whipping his anger into a frenzy of revenge. It wasn't until he woke amongst the prickles of a gorse bush that he realized he must have collapsed, exhausted, and slept.

Yesterday he had felt like a king. He had been ready to step into the shoes of the Lord of Mellin Cove. Today he had nothing but his anger. It was something he needed to hang on to. As long as his anger raged, he would not be defeated.

It was barely light when he stumbled over the rough ground and onto the cliff path. His direction was aimless, so he was taken by surprise when the harbour came into view far below.

Nothing was stirring. The families in the quayside cottages would still be asleep. As he watched, his eye was taken to a movement out at sea. He peered into the mist, focusing on the dark sails of a lugger. The Mellin Cove fleet was returning. He sank down in the bracken, not wanting to be seen silhouetted against the lightening sky.

As the boats sailed silently through the harbour entrance and on to their places on the quay, soft shafts of light began to slant over the cobbled harbour top. Women were emerging from their cottages now, some rolling up their sleeves, other pulling woollen shawls closer to themselves against the wind. Enor's brow creased in a frown, trying to understand what was going on. The women had formed a little group, waiting as the boats tied up and their men jumped ashore. Enor blinked. Annie was out there, and so was Jory. He'd assumed the women were going to meet their menfolk back from the sea, as seemed to be the habit hereabouts. But this was different. He could feel the hairs stand up on the back of his neck as he peered down on the activity.

The crowd seemed to have collected around one boat — Jem Pentreath's *Sally P*, if he was not mistaken. The figures seemed to be forming themselves into a rough line stretching towards the far end of the harbour. Objects were being lifted from the boat and passed to those on the quay. Enor watched, fascinated, as the items were passed from hand-to-hand. Snatches of conversation drifted up to him.

'Careful, man. No burst kegs tonight.'

'This one's heavy.'

'Catch it, Daniel.'

Enor threw his hands over his head as the realization dawned. They were smuggling! And the whole village was involved. He knew that if he bided his time, what he was witnessing could turn into the very ammunition he needed against this village. Now he saw an opportunity to get his own back on the whole of Mellin Cove, while earning a nice reward for himself at the same time.

Lanyon Manor was not difficult to find. Even by Enor's recently elevated standards, it was a grand place. His palms were sweating, but why? He was doing someone a favour. Sir Bartholomew Trevanion would thank him. More importantly, he would reward him. He took a deep breath and pulled the bell. It was some time before he was shown into the mine owner's sumptuous study.

The man looked up from his desk. 'I understand you have important information for me?'

Enor nodded and stepped forward. 'The thing is, sir — I saw how the Mellin Cove people treated you and your daughter, Lady Carolyn, in the churchyard that day. You had taken the trouble to pay your respects to that poor dead farmer, and they just turned on you. It was a disgrace.' He dropped his gaze in what he hoped was a suitably respectful gesture. 'I admired the dignity with which you handled the situation. You did not deserve to be treated with such disrespect.'

Trevanion glared out at him from under bushy white eyebrows. 'And just what business is that of yours, boy?'

Enor looked down at his feet again and tried not to shuffle them. 'I have learned something that might be of interest to you, sir. Something that will leave those people in no doubt that they cannot treat a man of your quality like that.'

'What are you talking about?' Trevanion snapped impatiently. 'I don't have all day, man. What is this thing you have learned?'

Enor cleared his throat. 'It's about smuggling, sir. I have reason to believe the people of Mellin Cove are involved in smuggling.'

'Well, of course they are. I know that. Is this your important information?' He stared at Enor from under a lowered brow. 'There's hardly a fishing village in Cornwall that is not involved in the despicable trade. The authorities also know this. It's catching them with the goods that's the problem.'

An image flashed into Enor's mind of the villagers unloading Jem Pentreath's boat. He'd seen them passing kegs of brandy and bolts of silk from hand to hand all the way up to the cave in the hill behind the harbour cottages. No more would these people spurn him. Enor smiled. 'What if I could help you there? Tell you where they hide their booty?'

Sir Bartholomew sat up. 'You know this?'

'I do, sir. I could take you there.'

The man studied him for a moment. Why should he trust this person? He knew nothing about him. And why was he so concerned about upholding the law? A frown creased his brow. 'You are not from Mellin Cove?' Enor shook his head. 'And yet you have an axe to grind against these people? Why is that?'

'I hate injustice, Sir Bartholomew. And the behaviour I witnessed towards you and the Lady Carolyn was a great injustice.'

Trevanion pursed his lips and continued to give Enor a hard stare. 'You say you know where these smuggled goods are hidden?'

'I do, sir.'

'Then come on, man.' He got to his feet. 'What are we waiting for?'

Enor had timed his visit to Lanyon Manor for late afternoon. If things went his way, then they needed to approach the cove after dark.

His plan couldn't have gone better. A mount from Sir Bartholomew's stables had been provided for him, and a trusted servant instructed to ride with them. It was late evening when the three reached the path that led down to the cove. 'We must leave the horses here,' Enor whispered, dismounting. 'A voice could carry on a still moonlit night like this, so we must be as quiet as possible.'

The three made their way down the winding track. Enor pointed towards the Rosens' cottage. Candles flickered in the kiddley, and they could hear raucous laughter from within.

'There is no way we can pass that place without being seen,' Sir Bartholomew hissed. 'You've brought us on a false mission.'

'I never said it would be easy, sir, but it can be done. Follow me, and keep low.' The fishing boats tied along the quay swayed in unison as waves lapped against their hulls. The men crept past the row of cottages, ducking into the shadows as they approached the kiddley. 'The cave is thirty yards ahead and up the hill,' Enor whispered. 'Follow me.'

No one emerged from the kiddley to discover their presence, and soon they were scrambling up the rocky hillside and into the black hole of the cave entrance.

'Is this it?' Sir Bartholomew said, squinting into the darkness. 'I can't see anything.'

'Our eyes will soon grow accustomed

to this dark. Over here . . . at this end . . . this is where they stowed the kegs of brandy, and the bales of silk and crates of tea I saw.' He moved forward. 'We must feel our way.' Enor had reached the back of the cave and felt around in the blackness. 'They were here . . . just here!' But all he could find was empty space. He was beginning to panic.

'You have brought us here under false pretences, sir. I take a dim view of this.' Sir Bartholomew was struggling to keep his rage under control. 'You have exposed me to danger. Was this your intention all along? Have you led us into a trap?'

'Of course not. How could you think that? This cave was full of smuggled contraband this morning. I saw it.' There was a catch in his voice. 'They must have moved it.' He didn't see Sir Bartholomew nod his silent instruction to his servant, but he felt the explosion of pain in his head as the blows rained down on him again and again. He was on his knees, shielding his head with his arms, and still the blows came. It was the repeated kicks in the ribs that had him crashing to the floor before he sank into unconsciousness.

# 14

Since she and Hal had become friendly, Wenna was spending more time down at Mellin Cove. Annie and Jory were happy for her to spend the occasional night under their roof, but they wouldn't accept her offer to work in the kiddley by way of thanks.

Neither of Wenna's friends had been aware that she had slipped out of the cottage that night; they were too busy keeping their customers in order at the kiddley. The place was attracting business from all over the moors now, and although some of their customers looked less than respectable, the couple offered hearty food as well as ale and kept a good, honest house.

Wenna stood on the quay listening to the lively babble emanating from the little makeshift tavern, and wondered why the families in the neighbouring cottages didn't complain. But then, if the menfolk in the cove supplied half of the kiddley's customers, why would they?

A sudden movement caught her eye and she stared into the darkness. Three shadowy figures were creeping along the front. Wenna ducked back behind the harbour wall, watching them. Her first thought was that they were intent on damaging the fishing boats tied up along the quay, but they crept on past them. She gazed after them. What were they up to? As if on cue, the moon slid from behind the clouds, making a silvery pattern on the water. It was only for a few seconds, but long enough for Wenna to recognize two of the men she was watching. She kept the moving shapes in sight until they had passed the kiddley and disappeared into the gloom on the far side of the harbour.

They had to be up to no good, but it wasn't her business. It was Annie and Jory's business, though. She knew she had to tell them. She glanced back to the kiddley. The noise wasn't exactly raucous, but the volume had increased. Those inside were clearly enjoying their ale. She smiled and thought, not for the first time, that if this had been Boscawen Harbour, she would have felt anything but safe; but here in Mellin Cove it was hard to imagine anything bad happening.

Wenna didn't hear the footsteps coming up behind her, so when the voice spoke over her shoulder she turned, startled. Her heart began to hammer when she saw Hal standing there.

'What are you doing here?' he said. 'Don't you know you shouldn't be wandering around the harbour at this time of night?' He glanced back to the lighted windows of the kiddley. 'Men don't always behave right when their bellies are full of ale. It's not safe for you to be here.'

It was dark, but there was still enough light to see that he was staring at her with a quizzical expression. For a second Wenna felt a flash of anger. She liked Hal — more than liked him; but it didn't give him the right to speak to her like that. She would decide what was safe for her, not he.

'And I suppose you are not one of these men with too much ale in his belly?'

'I may have supped a pint, but there are some in there that have downed six or more.' He was staring, not quite able to believe that this young woman was out here wandering about the harbour on her own at this time of night. 'What are you doing out here?' he asked again.

Wenna started and he saw her draw back. His tone had been a lot sterner than he'd intended. He tried to force some gentleness into his voice, but it wasn't a quality Hal was all that familiar with. Gentleness wasn't necessary when out ploughing the fields along the top end of Gribble Farm. He had no skills around women. But Wenna wasn't a woman. With her huge, innocent blue eyes, she could hardly be more than fifteen. She looked vulnerable, and his instinct was to protect her.

'No harbour is a safe place in the dark at night,' he said. 'What are you doing down here, Wenna?'

She could feel herself bristling. He was treating her like a child again. She flashed him an indignant glare. 'I'm not your responsibility, Hal.'

'It's not safe here. You should get yourself home.' He paused, still watching her. He couldn't see her properly here in the dark, but he recalled that tilt to the head, the determined stance, and a smile crossed his face. Once again she reminded him of himself at her age. He hadn't wanted to be fifteen back then; he'd wanted to be a man.

'Are you living with the Rosens now?'

'Not exactly,' Wenna hedged. Hal knew all about her grandmother, but he had assumed she was some kind of a gipsy woman. He probably thought the two of them lived together in a caravan. She didn't dare think about what he would say when he learned the truth.

Hal's eyes travelled to the raucous singing now coming from the tavern. 'Do Annie and Jory know you are wandering about out here?'

Wenna had to stop herself from stamping her foot in anger. 'I'm not wandering about. I stepped outside for a moment to get some air. I wasn't expecting to be accosted by you.' As soon as the silly words were out, she felt ridiculous.

'You think I am accosting you?' Hal's voice rose, but there was more than a hint of laughter in it. 'I can assure you, young Wenna, that I have no intention of accosting you or anyone else. I was concerned for your safety. But I can see you need no assistance from me.'

He had started to walk away when a movement from the end of the harbour caught his eye. In one reflex action he grabbed Wenna's arm and pulled her into the shadows.

Startled, Wenna almost let out a cry, but Hal put a finger to her mouth, shushing her. He had drawn her so close to him that she was sure he must feel her heart thudding.

And then she saw what had alerted him: two figures stealing through the darkness. She screwed up her eyes, staring out at them, but she was in no doubt. This was the same pair she'd seen before, but this time Annie's great-nephew wasn't with them. So where had he gone? If he'd passed her on the harbor, she would surely have noticed.

He could have slipped back into the cottage without her seeing him. If she mentioned this to Hal, she might be getting Enor into trouble — not that she cared much about that. Even though they had stayed under the same roof on more than one occasion, they had hardly shared two words. But any blame attributed to him might reflect on Annie.

'Did you get a good look at them?' Hal's voice was a harsh whisper.

'I'm not sure. Maybe.'

''Maybe' is good enough. Who did

you think you recognized?'

'I couldn't be absolutely certain,' Wenna said. 'But the big one looked like the man in the churchyard that day.' She paused. 'I think he was at your father's funeral.'

The two figures had cleared the harbour now, and Wenna could hear the sound of horses galloping off.

'Trevanion,' Hal said, glancing back in the direction of the cave.

The agent from Penzance had collected the contents in the early hours of the morning, but he was in no doubt that the mine owner had been in the cave and had expected to find it full of smuggled contraband. Someone had betrayed the people of Mellin Cove. But who?

He felt Wenna shiver beside him and looked down at her. The fear in her eyes made him want to embrace her; to stroke her hair and tell her nothing bad would happen to her as long as he was here to protect her.

He cleared his throat. 'I think you

should go indoors now,' he said, his voice guttural. 'It's getting cold out here.'

Wenna didn't argue, but she turned back as she reached the cottage door. Hal was already making his way up the hill out of Mellin Cove.

* * *

It was the children who found him the next day. Trudy and Ben Cope had been playing at the entrance to the cave when a rabbit scurried past them. The little girl ran in after it, laughing excitedly into the darkness. But she was screaming when she ran out .... screaming for her mother. Ben ran after his sister, not sure why he was feeling so scared.

Mary Cope was scraping vegetables into a bowl of water when her terrified children tumbled into the kitchen.

'Ghost . . . it's a ghost,' little Trudy gasped.

Mary looked from one to the other.

'Ghost? Now don't be silly: There are no ghosts in Mellin Cove.' She raised an eyebrow at Ben, who was two years older than his sister. 'What is she talking about, Ben? What frightened your sister?'

Ben shrugged. 'Don't know. It was something in the cave.'

'Don't go back there, Ma,' Trudy pleaded, hanging on to her mother in terror. 'Don't go back to the ghost. He's in there . . . waiting to grab children,' she whispered. 'It's a ghost, Ma . . . a real ghost.'

'Show me,' Mary said, taking her child's hand and stepping out onto the harbour top.

'No, Ma! Don't make me go back there . . . there's a ghost!'

Mary frowned, turning to her son. 'Did you see this ghost?'

Ben nodded. 'Yes, Ma. It's there. Don't go back to the cave. It'll get us.'

Mary glanced around her. The harbourside was deserted. All the men were at sea. Her gaze fell on the

Rosens' cottage and she ran over to bang on the door. Jory opened it, frowning when he saw his neighbour's distress.

'The children say there's something in the cave. Can you come with us to have a look, Jory?'

The little girl began tugging away from her mother. 'I'm not going back. Don't make me go back, Ma.'

Annie came out behind her husband and held out a hand to Trudy. 'I've just made some ginger biscuits, and I know how you love them. You and your brother come with me. I might find some milk to go with them.'

Mary gave her a grateful nod, and the children followed Annie into her warm kitchen.

'What's happened?' Wenna said, pushing back a tangle of pale hair as she emerged from the tiny back room.

'It's something about the cave,' Annie replied. 'Jory's gone with Ben and Trudy's mother to find out.'

'Do you think they might need some

help?' Wenna said, already on her way to the door.

'I doubt if you can do anything. Stay here where it's nice and warm,' Annie called after her. But the words came too late, for Wenna was already out the door and running along the harbour. This had to have something to do with the unsavoury characters she'd seen the previous night, she decided. She caught up with Jory and his neighbour at the end of the harbour.

'You don't think there really is a ghost in there, do you?' Mary Cope sounded worried.

Jory laughed. 'No, I don't. Whatever is in that cave, I can guarantee it is not a ghost. Stay here with Wenna while I have a look.' He walked into the cave, moving forward with caution. They heard his gasp from outside as his foot struck the body.

'Wenna! Run back and get some help. There's an injured man in here. We need something we can use as a stretcher, and some candles. Mary! You come in here to help me.'

Wenna tore back onto the harbour top, frantically knocking on doors. That was when she spotted Hal's cart rumbling down the hill towards her. She called out to him, desperately trying to wave him down. 'We need help,' she gasped. 'Back in the cave — an injured man.'

She jumped aside as the cart, laden with produce for the Rosens' kiddley, swept past at speed. She ran after it, catching her shawl and clutching it around herself before the wind took it.

Hal had brought the cart to a halt outside the Rosens' cottage before leaping down, clutching a board from the back. 'Fetch a lamp from Annie,' he called out to her as he tore up the hill to the cave.

At first Jory had thought the man to be dead, but when he put a hand on his chest he felt it rise — not much, but at least he was breathing. It wasn't until Hal ran in, closely followed by Wenna holding a lamp, that he began to suspect the injured man was Enor.

'Is he dead?' Wenna whispered.

'Near enough by the looks of him,' Hal said.

'He's not dead. I can feel a pulse,' Jory said. 'But we must get him out of here. He's lost a lot of blood.'

Carefully the men manoeuvred Enor onto the board from Hal's cart. Wenna held the lamp aloft as Mary laid a hand on the young man's brow.

'I think he has a temperature,' she said, walking beside the little procession as it made its way back to the harbour.

Wenna ran ahead to warn Annie about her injured great-nephew and took the children out the back door so as to spare them seeing the man's injuries. 'He's been badly beaten,' she whispered to Annie behind her hand. 'I think you should prepare yourself.'

Mary had gone round to the back door of the cottage to collect the children and take them home, while Hal and Jory carried Enor into the small front room.

'We need lots of hot water and strips of cotton we can use for dressings,' Jory said.

Annie put her hand to her mouth when she saw the badly beaten and bruised face of the injured man. 'Who could have done such a terrible thing?'

Wenna and Hal exchanged a look, but the slight lift of his eyebrow told her not to mention the men they had seen skulking about the harbour the previous night.

Annie and Wenna worked on Enor's injuries as the two men looked on. 'I feel so helpless,' Jory said to Hal. 'We need to find out who's done this. I know Enor did not make himself popular in Mellin Cove, but he didn't deserve such punishment.'

Hal stared at him. 'You're not suggesting that anyone from the cove did this?'

'Well, who else could it have been?'

Wenna looked up and saw the anger in Hal's eyes. She'd been about to speak when he put up a hand to silence her. She saw the muscles in his jaw working. 'The person who did this to young Vingoe will not go unpunished,' he said. 'I can promise you that.'

They made a bed up for Enor in the front room; and as Annie and Jory busied themselves with tidying up after the traumatic event, Wenna followed Hal out to the harbour.

'Why did you not let me speak? We both know who was responsible for this,' she said.

'And he will be dealt with,' Hal answered.

'It sounds very much like you will be putting yourself in danger, and then we will have another battered body to look after, if not a corpse.'

He stared at her, and then his face creased into a grin. 'You have a charming turn of phrase for someone so young. But please don't worry about me. There is more than one way to deal with a bully.'

# 15

Kit looked up from the design sketches he was studying and narrowed his blue eyes at the approaching visitor. 'Hal! This is a surprise. We don't often see you down here.' The industrious tapping noises that reverberated around the small boatyard stilled for a moment as curious workers looked up and watched the visitor join the yard owner in the wooden cabin that was the hub of the yard's business. 'I take it this isn't a social visit!'

'Something's happened and Jem's at sea. I thought you would want to know.'

Kit waited.

'It's Enor Vingoe. He's been badly beaten . . . could've been dead by now if some young 'uns down the cove hadn't come on him.'

'Beaten?' Kit sat up, his mind racing over events of recent days. Dewi had a proposal to rid them of the man, but that hadn't involved trying to kill him. 'Who attacked him?' he said grimly.

'I don't know for sure, but Trevanion and one of his men were creeping about the harbour late last night.' He paused and sighed. 'The thing is . . . Vingoe was found in the cave. Thankfully it was empty, but my guess is they expected to find certain goods in there.'

Kit put down his pen and sat back in his chair, frowning. 'You think Vingoe knew what the cave was used for?'

Hal shrugged. 'Why not? He was lodging with the Rosens.'

'Annie and Jory wouldn't have told him.'

'They wouldn't have needed to. He could have seen the boats being unloaded and watched for where the things were taken.'

'So what was Trevanion's part in this?'

'My thoughts would be that Vingoe went to him to betray the people. We all know that he was not very fond of

Mellin Cove or of the folk who live there, not after you made nonsense of his claim to the Hall. A man who is in that frame of mind can do some unconscionable things.' He glanced out to where the shell of a new fishing boat was taking shape on the blocks. 'Is that Jem's new lugger?'

Kit followed his gaze and smiled. 'It is. She'll be a fine boat. Your brother's fleet is growing.'

Hal nodded. Only weeks ago he would have been envious of Jem's success, and restless with a longing to have that life at sea for himself. He didn't know when the change of mind had taken place, only that he now knew beyond doubt that his future was on the land — and especially at Gribble Farm. It was a good feeling.

'Trevanion is not popular in the cove,' Kit said. 'Men like him thrive on respect, whether that is earned or not. Running a badly maintained mine where men were allowed to die because of his neglect warrants little respect.'

'And remember, there was that scene with him in the churchyard when he and his daughter turned up for my father's funeral.'

Kit did remember. He was trying to work things out. 'You think Enor went to him with the smuggling story?'

Hal nodded. 'Wenna told me she had seen three men acting suspiciously around the harbour area last night.' He stopped and met Kit's eyes. 'The third man was Enor Vingoe.'

Kit let out a long sigh. It was all very clear now. 'Vingoe wouldn't have known the agent had collected the goods early. He would hardly have been expecting to find the cave empty.'

Hal nodded. 'Trevanion may have thought Enor was leading him into some kind of trap. Who knows?'

Kit stood up and began to pace the floor. 'Could Enor still die?'

Hal frowned. 'Maybe. He was not in a good way when I last saw him.'

'We need to discuss this with Jem. It is time Sir Bartholomew Trevanion was made to pay for his actions.'

* * *

It was the next morning before the fleet returned, and the luggers had more than herring in their holds.

'Good night's work?' Hedra asked, giving her husband a knowing smile as he jumped onto the quay and swept her into a hug.

'Better than good this time,' he whispered into her hair. 'Do you see how happy all of them look?'

Hedra glanced around at the smiling faces of the boat crews as they greeted their womenfolk. 'I'm glad,' she said. 'The families deserve to have good food on their tables.' She stood on tiptoe to look over her husband's shoulder. 'Can you leave the others to unload the catch just this once, Jem? Kit and Hal are waiting back at Penhalow to speak with you.'

Jem raised an eyebrow. 'What has happened now?'

'I'll leave the telling to them, but there are things you should know about.' She glanced back at the Rosens' cottage as they left the harbour arm in arm. Their door hadn't opened like the others to welcome the return of the fleet. She bit her lip, hoping Enor Vingoe had not died in the night.

Kit and Hal were waiting for them in the parlour. Jane had provided them with tea, and there was an untouched plate of biscuits on the table. They both got to their feet as Jem and Hedra entered the room. A baby's cry drifted down to them from upstairs, and Hedra excused herself as she went to attend to the child.

'I'm intrigued,' Jem started. 'What is this all about?'

Kit and Hal recounted the story, with both men contributing. Jem listened with an expression of growing shock. 'How is young Vingoe now?' he asked when they had finished. 'Have you heard?'

'I called in on the Rosens early this

morning,' Kit said. 'There had been a slight improvement overnight, but he is in a lot of pain. Annie suspects that several of his ribs have been broken.'

'And I plan to call in on them when I leave here,' Hal said. He knew Wenna had sent word to her family that she would be staying on another night to help Annie and Jory with an unexpected family illness. She hadn't told them the real story.

'The thing is, what do we do about Trevanion?' Kit said. 'He will just continue with his violent ways unless he's stopped.'

'Isn't it more than that?' Hal looked from Kit to Jem. 'The man knows the place where we stored the goods. I think we can expect the revenue men to be breathing down our necks now.'

'Hal has a point,' Kit said. 'We need to find another safe place. The Hall is available if need be.'

'Would it not be safer to stop bringing the packages in for the time being? If the revenue men really are watching the cove, then we have to be careful,' Hal said.

Jem went to the brandy decanter, poured three glasses, and handed them round. 'It's too late for that,' he said. 'We brought in a new cargo this morning. It's still in the bottom of the boats.'

'In that case,' Kit said, 'it really has to be brought up to the Hall. We can't risk taking it back to the cave. But we need to wait until after dark.'

'But if we are already being watched . . . ' Hal cut in.

'We will need a distraction.' Jem was frowning into his glass.

'We could threaten Trevanion and tell him we will contact the authorities to make a safety examination of his mine if he goes to the authorities about the cave,' Hal suggested.

'I imagine he is well-practiced at squirming out of things like that,' Jem said.

Kit took a long sip of his brandy. 'We could round up the Mellin Cove men and march to Lanyon Manor.'

'And do what?' Hedra said, coming into the room. 'Beat the man up? Would that not make us as bad as he?'

Jem sighed. 'Hedra's right.' He turned to his wife. 'Do you have a suggestion to make?'

Hedra smiled. 'As a matter of fact, I do.'

The three men shared a look. 'Well, don't keep us guessing,' Kit said. 'What is this plan?'

Hedra felt the teapot and decided the contents were still warm enough to drink. She poured some tea into one of the spare tea bowls on the tray and lifted it to her lips. 'Now,' she said, settling herself into a chair, 'this is what we will do . . . '

* * *

Wenna was sitting on a stool by the makeshift cot bed that had been made for Enor in the Rosens' small front room. She was bathing the cuts on his forehead with damp strips of cotton torn from her petticoat. She looked up as Hal came in, and was annoyed when she felt a flush creep into her cheeks.

'How is the patient?' he asked, smiling down at her.

'He has been sleeping most of the time, which is good, because I think he will have much pain when he wakes properly.'

Despite himself, Hal felt compassion for the man. 'Has he said anything?'

Wenna shook her head. 'Not a word.'

'Nursing injured men in Mellin Cove seems to be becoming a constant pastime for you.' He was thinking of the day they had turned Mellin Hall's great front room into an emergency hospital as they tended to the wounded crewmen from the *Southern Star*. He remembered thinking at the time that a child such as she shouldn't be amongst so much blood and distress; but then she had played her part as much as any of the other helpers, just as she was doing now.

'Is there anything I can do?' he asked as Annie came into the room.

'You can take Wenna home. She has been looking after Enor for most of the night.'

'No, really, I'm fine,' Wenna protested. Going back to Boscawen House was the last thing she wanted to do, especially not now that Hal was here. And him taking her there was certainly not a good idea. She had no idea how he would react if he discovered she was actually Lady Rowenna Quintrell, and not the rather ragged urchin that she must look today.

Annie raised an eyebrow. 'You know how your father worries when you are away from home.'

That was true. Her father did worry. But he was still in London, and her grandmother and stepmother were not so caring. She smiled at Annie. 'I will go home today, Annie, but perhaps a little later.'

Annie turned her attention to Hal. 'Have you found out any more about who would do this to Enor?' she asked.

He frowned. It struck him that she, and perhaps the entire cove, would be suspecting that Kit had had a hand in the attack. He didn't want to mention Trevanion's part in it, but he had to say something. 'I've been discussing it with Kit and Jem. They are both as shocked as you. Enor did not make himself popular with Kit, it is true, but Kit would never have wished such violence on him. No one in Mellin Cove would have been involved in that.'

'Well, someone was,' Jory said, appearing from the kitchen and staring down at Enor's damaged face.

Hal glanced at Wenna's furrowed brow and guessed she was remembering what she had witnessed the previous night. She must be wondering why he was not mentioning it. He cleared his throat. 'It's a fine, bracing morning for a stroll across the moors. You look like you need the roses putting back in your cheeks, Wenna.'

'Now that is the best suggestion I've

heard all morning,' Annie said. 'Fetch Wenna's shawl from the kitchen, Jory. It will be chilly up there on the cliff path.'

'Am I to have no say in this plan?' Wenna laughed.

'Only if it's to agree what a good idea it is.' Hal grinned back.

'There you go,' Annie said, draping the grey woollen shawl over Wenna's shoulders. 'Get some fresh air into your lungs. I'll take care of Enor.'

Wenna allowed herself to be led from the cottage and walked with Hal up the winding path to the cliff top. They paused where the path split in opposite directions. Ahead was the drive that led to Mellin Hall. The junction to the right would take them past Gribble Farm. They turned left and walked out past the church.

'Why did you not tell them who we saw last night?' Wenna asked quietly, following his glance across the low stone wall to the freshly dug grave where his father's body lay.

'They will be told,' he said. 'But not

until we have decided how to deal with this.'

'We?' Wenna questioned. 'Who is we?'

'Jem and Kit, and perhaps some of the men from the cove.'

'I hope you are not considering more violence,' Wenna said, her voice rising in alarm.

Hal shook his head. 'No, that is not the plan.'

'And can you share this plan with me?'

He stopped suddenly and turned to her. For a moment she thought he was going to take her hands in his, but he didn't. 'It is best if you are not involved.'

'But I *am* involved,' she protested. 'I was there when Enor's poor beaten body was found in that cave. And I saw those men at the harbour last night, just as you did. It is not fair to leave me out of it.'

Hal sighed, narrowing his eyes against the wind as he stared out to sea. The horizon had misted over and there was rain in the air. He didn't want to put this young woman in danger, but then Hedra's plan was clever. He smiled at the memory of the earlier conversation. If Hedra were right — and none of them had doubted it — Lady Carolyn was having a dalliance with one of Sir Bartholomew's married servants.

'Everyone knows Carolyn has no shame when it comes to stealing another woman's man,' she'd told them. Hedra was remembering the shameful way the woman had gone after Kit — and even now, when she knew he was happily married to Dewi, she was still trying to seduce him at every encounter.

Kit had asked why Trevanion would care if his daughter was carrying on with a servant. Hedra had said, 'But what if that man were his favourite servant, Tom Swayne?'

Hal repeated the conversation to Wenna. 'What does this man look like?' she asked.

'I don't know him, but Hedra said he is a big, brawny brute of a man.'

'I wonder if he is bald.'

'According to Hedra, the man is as bald as a coot. Why do you ask?'

Wenna narrowed her eyes, trying to remember exactly what she'd seen the previous night. 'I believe I may have seen that man. Your description sounds very much like the man who accompanied Sir Bartholomew before Enor was attacked.'

Hal's eyes narrowed as he tried to remember the shadowy figures that had crept past. He'd recognized Trevanion but hadn't seen his companion clearly. 'You think this is the man who attacked Vingoe?'

Wenna shrugged. 'I can't say for sure, of course, but Hedra's description certainly sounds like Sir Bartholomew's companion.'

'I think you should tell the others about this,' Hal said. 'We could walk over that way now if you like.'

'Why not? I would like to help.'

They walked in companionable silence for a few minutes and then Hal said, 'I suppose we should make a definite decision over what to do about your grandmother's little haul. We need to tell Jem and Hedra about your idea of giving back to the community.'

Wenna sighed. 'It is the only thing that makes sense. Grandmother won't like it, but that is just too bad. She wouldn't like going to prison either, so she has no choice but to agree to whatever is decided.'

Hedra's face broke into a smile when she saw them on her doorstep.

'Wenna has something interesting to tell you about Mr Swayne,' Hal said.

'Really? Well, do come in. Dewi is here. We were just about to have some tea.'

They began to follow her into the parlour, but Hedra put up a hand to Hal. 'Sorry,' she said, grinning. 'But this is ladies only.'

'What are you scheming?' he asked, amused.

'You will find out in good time, Hal. Just call back in an hour or so to collect Wenna. We should be finished by then.'

He looked at Wenna. 'Is that all right by you?' She nodded. 'Very well. I'll call back in an hour.'

Dewi patted the chair next to her. 'Come in and sit down, Wenna. You look exhausted.'

Hedra settled herself too. 'Hal said you had information for us?'

'I don't know for sure,' Wenna began. 'But that servant he told me about — Tom Swayne, the one who seems to know Lady Carolyn rather well — I think he is the one who attacked Enor Vingoe.'

Dewi sat back in her chair and stared at her. 'Really?'

'Swayne is a big, brawny character with a polished scalp in place of hair,' Hedra said.

Wenna nodded. 'That is an exact description of the man I saw with Enor and Sir Bartholomew at the harbour last night.'

'If that's true, it may even strengthen my plan,' Hedra said, turning to Dewi. 'How would you feel about inviting Lady Carolyn to tea?'

Dewi squinted at her, frowning. 'I would not be happy about it. How would that help?'

'Never mind that for now. Would she accept your invitation?'

'I have no idea. She may do if she is intrigued enough about my motive for suggesting the visit.'

Hedra pursed her lips, thinking. 'That's not enough. We have to be sure she would go to Mellin Hall.'

'The only way of ensuring that would be if Kit asked her,' Dewi said.

'Of course,' Hedra said, beaming. 'The invitation must come from Kit!'

'Kit would never do that,' Dewi said, giving her sister-in-law a shocked look.

'But you could persuade him,' Hedra said, her mischievous grin widening.

Dewi threw up her hands. 'I still don't understand. Even if she comes to Mellin Hall, what happens then? What is it you expect me to do?'

'Not you, Dewi . . . well, not just you.' Hedra threw a glance at Wenna. 'All three of us. We will all be there. It will be a genteel taking of tea, during which Lady Carolyn will learn how much we know about her.' She gave a little exaggerated cough. 'Her . . . *activities*. We will start with the least offensive things and build up to the most shocking revelations that she will certainly not want to be made public.'

'Do we know of such things?' Dewi asked with wide-eyed innocence.

'We already know of a few, but if we make it our business to discover more outrageous dalliances that she has been involved in, then we will be in a position of power.'

'I don't see how that would stop Sir Bartholomew from telling the authorities about the cove's smuggling activities,' Dewi said, and she put a hand to her mouth in embarrassment.

'Smuggling activities?' Wenna exclaimed. 'Is that what this is all about?'

'Sorry, Hedra. I didn't mean to say that,' Dewi said. 'But if Wenna is to be one of us now, then we need to trust her.' She turned to Wenna. 'You will not say anything, will you?'

Wenna thought of her own even more scandalous secret about her grandmother, and shook her head. 'Of course I will not mention to anyone what you've just said. But it does now all make sense. Annie told me how Enor tried to claim he was the rightful owner of Mellin Hall. I must say, it shocked me.'

'Kit put him right on that,' Dewi said quickly.

'Yes, Annie told me the real story,' Wenna said. 'I have not known Enor very long, but I can imagine how very bitter he would have been when he learned his inheritance claim was groundless, and how he would desire to have revenge on not only the St Neots and Kit, but all the people of Mellin Cove.' She eyed the other two. 'From what I witnessed in the churchyard at the burial of Mr Pentreath, Sir Bartholomew would not have enjoyed being taken to task by the men. Presumably if he saw a way of getting back at them, he would.'

'Precisely,' Hedra said. 'Which is why I believe Enor went to him directly after meeting Kit and all of us at Mellin Hall to wreak his revenge on all of us by telling Trevanion about certain activities in the cove. Perhaps he even witnessed something — he lives right there in the Rosens' cottage, after all. If he happened to be there when the goods were unloaded, then he could easily have followed them to the cave.'

'It is hard not to believe the man got what he deserved,' Dewi said, and winced. 'Is that very terrible of me?'

Hedra smiled at her. 'Uncharitable, perhaps, but understandable.'

'So what do we do now?' Wenna said.

'I don't see how Carolyn's indiscretions could affect her father's decision to tell the authorities what he believes he knows about the cove.'

'Sir Bartholomew has a weakness.' Hedra looked from one to the other. 'His lovely daughter, Lady Carolyn. If she persuaded him not to do something, he would listen.'

'I am beginning to understand.' Wenna smiled.

'That's rather clever,' Dewi said. 'So if we let Carolyn know we will make her secret dalliance with her father's servant public knowledge, she will not be happy.'

'I suspect not.' Hedra's eyes twinkled. 'My belief is that she will do all she can to persuade us not to talk. The power will then lie with us.'

Wenna clapped her hands. 'I'm looking forward to this.'

Hal arrived to collect her just as he'd said. But Wenna was surprised that he had not brought his wagon. She'd assumed he would be taking her home.

'Are you hungry?' he asked, grinning down at her as they walked away from Penhalow. 'Ma usually makes tea about this time. Another one at the table will be no problem.'

It wasn't the most gracious invitation Wenna had ever received to dine with someone, but it was the most welcome. She was very hungry indeed.

'After we've eaten, I'll take you home.' He was looking at her, and she cast her eyes down.

'Thank you, Hal,' she said.

# 16

Wenna woke early the next morning and stretched luxuriously. She didn't know if the feeling of warm excitement surging through her was because she had arranged to see Hal again that day, or because of the growing plan to reverse her grandmother's treachery. If it worked, it would put the spoils of the woman's greed to a new and better use.

Wenna's head sank back into the feather pillow and she closed her eyes, going over the events of the previous day in her mind — and then it struck her. She sat up, pushing the tangle of pale hair from her face. No one had asked who her grandmother was!

Her story had shocked Hal so much that it hadn't occurred to him to enquire about Wenna's background. Or did he already know? Wenna had certainly never told him that she was

Lady Rowenna Quintrell. Could he have discovered it himself? And what about the St Neots — could they also know who she really was?

Wenna threw back the bed covers, swung herself down onto the woven rug, and began to pace the floor. Had all her efforts to conceal her true identity been in vain? Was it possible that her new friends had all been humouring her?

She suddenly felt afraid. When Hal had brought her back to Boscawen House the previous evening, she'd insisted on him dropping her at the end of the lane. Why hadn't he been curious about where she lived? Perhaps the day that stretched ahead was going to be more difficult than she thought.

* * *

Hal was up at first light to tend to the animals. The appetizing aroma of frying bacon filled the kitchen when he got back. His mother was piling the cooked rashers onto a plate and keeping them warm in the oven. She looked up and smiled as her eldest son came into the kitchen. 'I hope you're hungry,' she said. 'I may have overdone the helpings.'

She turned back to the cooking range so quickly that Hal knew she was hiding a tear. His mother was still making breakfast for six, when there were only five of them now. He went over and kissed her cheek.

She brushed him away with an embarrassed 'Be off with you,' and waved a spatula at him. 'Get off to the yard and wash some of that grime from your hands. Nobody sits at my table with dirty hands.'

'Always the bossy one,' Hal called back as he went out to the yard, but he was grinning.

'I like that young woman you've taken up with,' Sally said as he reappeared.

'Hardly a woman, Ma. Wenna's a child. And I certainly haven't *taken up* with her.'

His mother looked surprised. 'She's eighteen if she's a day. I wouldn't call that a child.' She was remembering how Wenna had looked at her son. Was he just covering his embarrassment, or was he really not aware that a lovely young woman had her eye on him? But Sally was also remembering how his brother Luk had flushed deeply when Wenna entered the room. And at twenty-one, he was more the girl's age.

Hal had tucked a couple of slices of ham between two chunks of his mother's bread. He bit into them and was wiping the crumbs from his mouth with the back of his hand. Sally sighed. Her eldest son would never be a gentleman, but he was a good worker and had a heart of gold. And whether he was aware of it or not, he was about to share that heart with a young woman he still believed was just a girl. 'You seem to be more settled these past few days, Hal,' she said.

'If you mean I'm not hankering after going to sea with Jem?' He screwed up his face. 'Maybe. I'm not sure.' But his mother was right. After the sudden death of his father, Hal had been thrust into his role as head of the family. It had put paid to any ideas he might have been considering about switching from the land to the sea. It had been a foolish notion, he knew that now. It was a good life on the farm. He was satisfied. Except . . .

His mind went back to Wenna. His mother was wrong. She *was* just a child, which was why he felt so protective of her. She was different though, he mused. She was educated. It had been impossible to imagine her at home with her family when she told him so little about them. He'd guessed her father to be a teacher; perhaps she was embarrassed at introducing a simple farmer like himself to an educated gentleman.

But then there was the grandmother. If she really was in league with pirates as Wenna had said, then she was no lady. It was confusing. Hal was rising from the table when Luk appeared. 'I need to slip away for an hour or two this morning,' he told his younger brother. 'Can you manage the top field on your own for bit?'

'If you mean can I plant a few tates in straight rows, then aye, I think I can manage that.'

Hal grinned down at him and teased, 'Don't work too hard, will you, young 'un.'

Luk reached for the bread knife. 'You seeing that girl again today?'

'Mind your business, little brother.' Hal laughed as he left the kitchen.

A soft rain had begun to fall as he rode up to the field of standing stones where he and Wenna had arranged to meet. He couldn't see her at first, but then his face broke into a wide grin as she appeared from behind one of the stones and gave him a wave.

Hal's heart gave a sudden lurch as he watched her tuck her sketchbook inside her blue cloak and hurry towards him. He wasn't used to this strange fluttery feeling deep inside him, so he frowned.

His 'good morning' came out with a gruff tone that he hadn't intended, so he said quickly, 'I brought Horace. I thought you might like to ride him back.'

Wenna shook her head. 'I'm happy to walk beside him. It's not far to Penhalow. What time did Kit and Dewi say they would meet us?'

'Mid-morning,' Hal said, his eyes on the mist rolling in from the sea. 'Jem hasn't taken the *Sally P* out today. He's entrusted that task to Daniel Carney. And I know Pascow Hendry was at the wheel of the *Bright Star* when she sailed out earlier.' He glanced down at her. 'I've asked Kit not to mention what we discussed before we get there. That story is best coming from you, Wenna. It's important that they fully understand.'

Wenna nodded. She had spent many waking hours the previous night thinking the whole thing through. But now she was certain that what she was suggesting was the right thing to do.

They walked either side of Horace, the mist of rain wetting their cheeks. Sally's words about Wenna being a woman kept running through Hal's head. It made him feel awkward. He wasn't comfortable around women. It had been fine when he'd believed Wenna to be a child . . . but a woman? This would make everything more difficult. The silence between them should have been easy and companionable, as it would be with friends. But this morning it felt different. It felt awkward.

Hal's stony expression was worrying Wenna. Was he now regretting his offer to help her with this scheme? Now that he'd had time to think it over, had he now thought better of it? She was becoming more depressed by the minute.

The rain had taken a serious hold by the time they reached Penhalow. Hedra opened the door and hurried them in. 'You're both soaked,' she sympathized, brushing down Wenna's wet cloak.

'Come into the warm. We have a fire going in the back room.'

Kit, Dewi and Jem were seated comfortably around the blazing fire, their cheeks pink from the heat. There was a tray of tea things on the table, but the men were drinking brandy. Jem got up to welcome Hal and Wenna, pulling out a chair for Wenna to sit.

'Would you like some tea?' Hedra offered.

Wenna shook her head. 'Thank you, no. I'm happy to just sit by the fire.'

Dewi smiled a greeting and touched Wenna's hand as she sat down next to her. Hal was provided with a glass of brandy, and Jem topped up his and Kit's glasses.

'Right,' Hedra said, dropping into a chair beside her husband, 'I'll absolutely burst if someone doesn't tell me soon what this is all about.'

Wenna slid Hal a nervous look. 'Could you start, Hal? You explain things much better than me.' Hal gave her a look that made her knees go weak.

She glanced away, embarrassed, giving herself a mental scolding. She would have to concentrate better than this. If she allowed her feelings to get the better of her, she would ruin everything.

'Well, where shall I start?' Hal said with a sigh. 'Perhaps we should go back to the day the *Southern Star* was wrecked.'

They all studied Jem's and Hedra's faces as the story unfolded. When Hal had finished, the room was silent.

Hedra looked stunned. She turned to Wenna. 'You're telling us that Lady Catherine Quintrell is a pirate?'

Hal was frowning at Wenna. 'I don't understand. Who is Lady Catherine Quintrell?'

Wenna could feel her cheeks flaming, and she bit her lip. 'Lady Catherine is my grandmother.'

Hal blinked. 'Your name's not Wenna at all, is it?' His tone was accusing.

Wenna squared her shoulders. 'I'm Lady Rowenna Quintrell. My father is Sir George Quintrell, and he is a

Member of Parliament. I don't live in a little cottage at the bottom of that lane where you dropped me off last night, Hal. My home is Boscawen House.' She looked at Hedra. 'How did you know?'

'I recognized you from that first moment at Mellin Hall. I saw you out in your carriage one day with your father and grandmother. Our fathers are acquainted.'

A stunned silence filled the room. Hedra touched her forehead. 'I'm so sorry, Wenna. I didn't realize the others were not aware of who you are.'

'It's fine,' Wenna said. 'It wasn't a secret.' She swallowed. 'I just felt people here might shun me if they knew who I was.'

'Why on earth would anyone do that?' Dewi exclaimed.

'My grandmother does not endear herself to people. I'm not proud to say it, but she can be quite spiteful at times — and now she has truly shamed me.' But even as she spoke, she knew that wasn't the real reason. Hal had assumed she was an ordinary girl. Now that he knew she was a lady — one of Cornwall's so-called gentry — he would feel uncomfortable around her. He would not trust her anymore. Whatever their relationship had been, it was now over. She stared miserably into the fire.

Dewi threw her hands in the air. 'I really don't see what difference this makes. The very fact that you want to return the valuables your grandmother stole demonstrates what a kind, honourable person you are.'

'I agree,' Kit said. 'What you have proposed is admirable, Wenna.'

'And that goes for us, too,' Jem said. Hedra nodded.

'So what do you say, brother? Are we all committed to this scheme?'

Wenna watched Hal drain his glass and put it on the table. 'You can count me in,' he said. She waited for him to glance across at her and smile. But he avoided her eyes. It was obvious that their friendship was at an end.

# 17

Kit was more than a little suspicious when Dewi suggested they should invite Carolyn Trevanion to take tea with them. 'I thought you detested the woman,' he said.

'Not detested, no. Admittedly, I do not consider her a close friend.'

'So what is this? Bridge-building?'

Dewi flashed him a brilliant smile. 'That's exactly what it is.' She moved round the table and slid her arms around his neck. 'You will invite her, Kit, won't you?'

Kit pushed his plate away and pulled his wife onto his knee, gazing at her and smiling. 'You do realize Carolyn will view such an invitation in a particular way, do you not?'

'Surely not if you put both our names on the invitation.'

Kit gave her a sideways look. 'You are

up to something. I can tell.'

Dewi kissed him on the cheek and gave him an innocent look. 'My husband is such a suspicious man. I cannot imagine why.'

'Hmm,' Kit said, still watching her. 'My sister would not have put you up to this, by any chance?'

'Just write the invitation, my love.' She wrinkled her nose at him. 'And trust me.'

* * *

Lady Carolyn Trevanion's carriage swung up to Mellin Hall the following Friday afternoon. Kit and Dewi were at the door to greet her. She gave Dewi a dismissive glance, concentrating her dazzling smile on Kit. She took the hand he offered and fluttered her eyelashes at him as she stepped down onto the stone flagging.

'We're so glad you could come. It seems such a long time since you visited us.' Dewi was trying for a conversational tone.

Lady Carolyn held her head high, making no attempt to respond. She allowed herself to be led into the vast hall, passing portraits of the Constantine family on the way. She had heard stories about an upstart who had attempted to make a claim on Mellin Hall and Kit's estate. If the tales were true, he had shown the infidel the door. The thought of that excited her, and then when his invitation to the Hall arrived she could hardly contain her pleasure.

Including his pushy little wife's name on the invitation was, she knew, a mere concession to social politeness. It was Kit who had wanted to see her — and she could guess why. Her mouth curved into a smile as she glanced up at his handsome profile. He was smiling too. The flutter of her heart beneath the satin bodice of her pale green gown was pleasurable.

Kit paused as they reached the double doors to the drawing room.

Carolyn saw his glance to Dewi. Was this the moment when he would dismiss the wretched girl? Her heart gave a sudden lurch at what she believed was the certain knowledge that he wanted to be alone with *her*.

The sight of his sister Hedra seated so comfortably by the fire made her swallow. What was she doing here?

'You know my sister-in-law,' Dewi said, coming forward. 'And this is my friend, Lady Rowenna Quintrell.'

Carolyn spun round, confused. This wasn't what she had been expecting.

Dewi produced her most charming smile. 'Please take a seat, Carolyn. I'll ring for tea in a moment.'

Carolyn sank into a chair. Her brow wrinkled as she looked from one to the other.

Before she could make sense of what was happening, Kit made a little bow. 'My apologies, ladies,' he said. 'I have been summoned down to the boatyard. Some emergency — trivial no doubt; but I should attend to it.' He moved forward and kissed Dewi on the cheek. Carolyn stiffened. 'I'd like to believe you ladies would miss me.' He grinned at each woman in turn. 'But I suspect that will probably not be the case.'

'Oh, be off with you, Kit.' Dewi laughed, and called after him as he reached the door, 'We'll save you some cake.'

Carolyn could feel an annoyed flush rising to her cheeks. She was getting the distinct feeling that she had been led into a trap. She scowled at the three women in turn. 'Can we drop the deception now? Why am I here?'

Hedra settled herself in her chair. She took her time, enjoying the woman's growing fury. 'Tom Swayne. I take it the name is familiar to you?'

'He is my father's servant.' Carolyn tilted her head, challenging her, but not before Hedra saw the wariness in the cold blue eyes.

Dewi also noticed it, and smiled. 'The thing is, Carolyn, we know all about your — how shall I put it? Your *friendship* with Mr Swayne.'

For a split second a look of blind panic flashed across the woman's face, and then her eyes sparked with rage. 'What are you suggesting?' She jumped to her feet and set off across the room towards Dewi, but Wenna jumped up and blocked her way.

Carolyn sidestepped her and rounded on Dewi. 'You have always hated me. Do you imagine I don't know how jealous you are of my friendship with Kit? We were close before you ever came on the scene.'

Wenna had tried to step in front of her again, but Carolyn pushed her aside. 'Everyone knows he married you for your family's money. You don't think he actually cares about you, do you?'

'Don't listen to her, Dewi. She's lying,' Wenna said. 'Everyone can see how much Kit adores you.'

Dewi blinked back an angry tear and faced up to Carolyn. 'You would love to believe that Kit once cared for you, would you not? But your vindictiveness will not work, not this time. And if you think you can avoid the truth about yourself and Mr Swayne, then you are mistaken. We know all about your secret trysts. Your gutter morals are well known around Mellin Cove.'

'How much does your father know, Carolyn?' Hedra put in.

The woman's look of fear was unmistakable. 'My father does not listen to lies,' she spat back.

'Not lies.' Hedra smiled. 'We have proof of what we say. You were seen, you and your lover, and by more than one person. They are quite prepared to report it all to Sir Bartholomew.' She paused and lifted an eyebrow. 'I cannot imagine he would be very pleased with either of you.'

'My father does not rule my life,' Carolyn thundered.

'Perhaps not, but he does pay your dressmaker's bill and provides you with the kind of privileged lifestyle few of the rest of us could afford.'

Carolyn rounded on Dewi. 'Is it money you are after? Is that what all this is about?'

Dewi shook her head. 'Not at all. I would not accept your crumbs even if I was starving.'

'Well, you clearly want something. What is it?'

Hedra got up and began to stroll around the room. 'We want to help you, Carolyn. We want to help you make sure your father never gets to hear about you and his devoted servant. You should be more appreciative of what we are trying to do for you.'

'I understand none of this. What are you talking about?'

'Wenna has a story to tell you. Sit down, Carolyn.' Hedra pushed her into a chair. 'And make yourself comfortable.'

Wenna took a breath. 'It all started two nights ago, when I was taking a stroll around the harbour. It was dark and I saw three figures moving through the shadows. They looked sinister, so I stepped out of sight. But then the moon came out from behind a cloud and for a moment the harbour was lit up.' She looked at Lady Carolyn. 'One of the men was your father. I recognized him from that time in the churchyard when you and he attended Mr Pentreath's funeral. The second man was Enor Vingoe, whom I know because I have stayed under the same roof as him in my friends' cottage. I didn't recognize the third person. He was a tall, broad man, and when the moon broke out for a second it shone on his head. He was completely bald.'

Carolyn stiffened. 'What does this have to do with me?'

'Tell her, Wenna,' Dewi said, watching Carolyn.

'The reason it is interesting,' Wenna went on, 'is because I saw the little group return from wherever they had been, but this time one of them was missing. Enor Vingoe was not with them. He was later found in a cave behind the harbour, more dead than alive. Your father and his servant had given him a cruel beating.'

Carolyn's eyes flew open. 'This is outrageous! You're lying. My father never gets involved in violence.'

'But your friend Mr Swayne does,' Hedra said. 'If I am not mistaken, Sir Bartholomew depends on his violent streak to keep him safe.'

'He also depends on his loyalty,' Carolyn snapped. The words were out before she could stop them. She could now see where this was going. She swallowed. 'Please don't tell my father about my friendship with Tom. He . . . he would not understand.'

'I imagine not,' Hedra said, glancing at the others.

Carolyn made fists of her hands. 'What is it you want me to do?'

'You tell her, Dewi. It will come better from you.'

Dewi met Carolyn's angry stare. 'We believe the reason the three of them were prowling about the harbour that night is because they believed they would discover illegal contraband in that cave. And when your father realized he had been misled, he took his fury out on the person who had guided him there — Enor Vingoe. You know as well as I do, Carolyn, how much your father hates the St Neots and the Pentreaths. In fact he hates the whole of Mellin Cove, and would do everything in his power to destroy all of us.'

Carolyn tilted her chin and glanced away.

'For that reason,' Dewi continued, 'we suspect Sir Bartholomew may tell the authorities that he actually did see contraband in the cave, and that the entire cove — including Mellin Hall — is engaged in the smuggling trade.'

Carolyn narrowed her eyes at Dewi. 'Would that be so far from the truth?'

'You are forgetting that you need our help, Carolyn,' Hedra interrupted.

Carolyn sighed. 'What is it that you want me to do?'

'We want you to dissuade your father from taking the story to the authorities,'

Dewi said, holding out her hands. 'That's all we are asking.'

They were all staring at Carolyn. For a moment Wenna thought she would jump up, brand them all as charlatans, and march out of the room. She swallowed, waiting.

Carolyn sat back in her chair, watching the three of them, and then her gaze settled on Dewi. 'Tell your servant to bring my carriage round. I will not be staying for tea.'

Dewi rang for Tomas. They all sat in silence as they waited for him.

'Lady Carolyn is leaving, Tomas,' Dewi informed him when he appeared. 'Can you bring her carriage round, please?'

He smiled. 'It's already at the door, Miss Dewi.' Out of the corner of her eye she saw Hedra's mouth twitch in a smile.

Carolyn stood. 'Your request will be attended to,' she said coldly as she swept out of the room.

'We did it.' Wenna laughed, clapping

her hands. 'We did it!'

Hedra put her fingers to her cheeks. 'I can't believe that was so easy.'

'Do you think she will keep her word?' Dewi asked.

'That depends on how much she wants us to keep her secret,' Hedra said. 'And I rather think Lady Carolyn wants that very much.'

* * *

The sun had risen over the moor, bathing everything in a mellow golden glow as Kit rode out the next morning. He narrowed his eyes at the recklessness of the rider he could see speeding towards him across the rough terrain and slowed Sabre to a trot, keeping the approaching horse and rider in his sights. He was curious. It was rare for him to see anyone on his early morning ride. It was then that he heard his name being called into the wind. He reined in his stallion as the stranger approached. Kit was wary.

His hand went to his pistol.

'Kit . . . Kit.' The rider's voice carried on the wind as the distance between them closed at speed.

He frowned. 'Carolyn?' He could hardly believe his eyes. Lady Carolyn Trevanion — the elegant, haughty woman who had so often attempted to flirt outrageously with him in the drawing room of Mellin Hall — had taken on the mantle of a wild creature. A brown leather doublet and breeches replaced her usual finery. Her normally carefully coiffured flax-coloured hair streamed out behind her, and she was not riding sidesaddle.

'Kit!' she gasped, struggling to catch her breath. 'I must speak with you.'

He was trying to control his shock at her obvious disarray. 'What on earth are you doing out here on the moors at this time of morning, Carolyn? It's not safe for a lady on her own.'

'Why do you imagine I dressed like this? Do I look like a lady? I knew I would find you out here. I have come to warn you,' she said breathlessly. 'It's about my father. Can we dismount for a moment?'

Kit jumped down from Sabre and helped Carolyn from her horse. They walked on, leading their mounts away from the track. 'About your father, you said . . . ' Kit started.

Carolyn pushed her hair out of her eyes and glanced around as though ensuring she would not be overheard on the deserted moor. 'You will know of the arrangement I had with your wife and sister and the Lady Rowenna Quintrell,' she said.

Kit cleared his throat. He had been amused when Dewi related the undertaking they had secured from Carolyn under the pretext of inviting her for tea the previous day. 'Go on,' he said evenly.

'I was to dissuade my father from going to the authorities with certain information he was in possession of.' She paused, biting her bottom lip. 'In exchange for a certain understanding.'

Kit nodded. 'But I was too late. My father has already passed on the information to the authorities.'

Kit stared at her. The fleet was due to make another landing that morning — and it was more than just a fishing catch. Now that the cave was no longer a safe store, they had settled on taking the goods to Mellin Hall. There was no time to lose. He had to get back to the cove to warn them.

Carolyn was still speaking. 'I needed all of you to know that this was none of my doing. I tried to keep my side of the bargain. I expect the ladies to keep theirs.'

But this woman's reputation was the last thing on Kit's mind. 'You must return home immediately, Carolyn, and see what more you can learn about this.' He was already starting to help her remount her horse.

'If you will allow me to finish,' she said crossly, 'I will tell you the rest. They will be sending the soldiers down to the cove after dark tonight to search some cave down by the harbour.' She took a breath and looked down at him. 'If they find nothing there, then they will search Mellin Hall. That was my father's suggestion.'

Kit's mind was reeling. Were the smuggled goods already at the Hall? If the soldiers turned up there after dark, it would be at exactly the same time as the agent was due to arrive to collect the goods. They would be caught red-handed. He could feel the panic starting inside him. He had to get back to alert everyone.

'I did my best, Kit. You *will* tell the others, won't you?'

'I'll tell them,' he said grimly, slapping the rump of her horse so that it took off at a gallop.

Kit tried to organize his thoughts as he raced across the moor. He had been in this exact situation once before, when a certain captain had brought a troop of redcoats to the Hall not long after he and Hedra had taken over the running of it. They had come on the pretext of warning them that smuggling was rife in the area and they believed illicit goods were being hidden locally. On that occasion the soldiers had searched all the cottages, but to no avail. He allowed himself a grim smile, remembering the mad scramble to help Jem and Hal load the contraband on the cart from Gribble Farm and trundle it up the hill to Mellin Hall.

But this time things were different. This time the soldiers would be searching the Hall! As Kit reached the top of the cove, he could see that the fishing fleet was already in the harbour. Did that mean the new cargo would already have been loaded? He guessed so. Under the circumstances, the men would have taken no chances with leaving it on board.

Tomas was in the yard to meet him, with his hands on his head at the speed Kit galloped in. He made a grab for Sabre's reins and ran a calming hand down the horse's sweat-soaked neck.

'Take care of him, Tomas, I had to ride him hard.'

'Is anything wrong, Master Kit?'

'Come into the Hall after you have attended to Sabre. I might need your help.'

Kit found Dewi in the small morning room, and she wasn't alone. Wenna looked up and smiled as he strode into the room. They both saw at once that something was wrong. Dewi jumped up and ran across the room. 'Whatever's happened, Kit?' Wenna was on her feet too now. Her hand went to her throat as he described his encounter with Lady Carolyn Trevanion on the moor.

'The soldiers are coming to search the Hall?' Dewi's eyes were wide with horror. 'But they'll find all the contraband.'

'Has it already been brought here?' Kit asked, but he hardly needed to wait for his wife's reply. 'We need to move it!'

Dewi nodded. 'That's why Wenna is here.'

'I wanted to help,' Wenna said. 'And now even more. Just tell me what I can do.'

'There's Penhalow,' Dewi suggested. 'Hedra and Jem would be willing to store the goods.'

Kit pursed his lips. 'The cottage is too small. If the soldiers searched it, they would discover the goods for sure.'

'Gribble Farm!' Wenna's expression ignited with excitement. 'No one would think of looking there, and there are plenty of sheds and outhouses where things could be hidden.'

Kit and Dewi exchanged a look. He shook his head. 'I'm not sure about putting Sally under such stress, not so soon after losing Sam.'

'Well, at least let me talk to Hal. I'm sure he will know what to do,' Wenna said.

Kit nodded. 'That's an idea. We need Hal and Jem up here at the Hall.'

Wenna was already heading for the door. 'I'll call in at Penhalow on the way to Gribble Farm,' she said as she hurried out.

# 18

Hedra and Jem were as shocked as she'd expected them to be when she told them the news.

'Carolyn Trevanion rode all the way across the moor to give Kit this information?' Hedra's expression was one of astonishment. 'But why did she not simply go to the Hall?'

'Because she knew Kit was out riding,' Jem said dryly. 'And it was he she wanted to see.'

Hedra shook her head. 'And now she wants us to honour our contract by not telling her father what his daughter is really like.'

'At least she has warned us,' Wenna said.

'Hmm . . . ' Hedra wasn't sure. 'If we can believe her, that is.'

'We need to speak to Kit,' Jem said.

'Will Jane look after the children until we return?'

Hedra nodded. 'But do not let us detain you, Wenna. Hal should know about this as soon as possible.'

Wenna left them making hurried arrangements to go to the Hall. She tore along the cliff path, arriving breathless at Gribble Farm. She couldn't see Hal in the field as she ran up and her heart sank. But then he appeared from the side of the farmhouse. His expression registered his surprise. He called out to her.

'I have news,' she gasped. 'Let me first catch my breath.'

'News of what? What has happened?'

'It's Sir Bartholomew. He has already informed the authorities about the extra cargo the boats bring in. Everyone is in trouble unless the items can be moved from Mellin Hall.'

'He's done what?' Hal exploded.

Wenna put a hand on his arm. 'Stay calm. We have time to deal with this, but we must act without delay. Can you come back with me to the Hall?' She glanced behind him to where his two younger brothers, Luk and Kadan, stood. 'Perhaps your brothers could come too?'

'Yes, of course,' Hal said, waving them across. He quickly explained the situation to them.

'We're wasting time here talking about it. Let's go,' Luk said.

'You two go ahead; Wenna and I will collect the wagon and meet you there,' Hal said quickly.

None of the Pentreath brothers bothered to collect jackets. The two younger ones began hurrying along the cliff path as Wenna followed Jem into one of the large farm sheds.

Tomas had been busy spreading the word amongst the men from the cove, and a large group of them were already at the Hall when Wenna and Hal rumbled up. Jem and Kit had taken charge and were organizing everyone into working parties to collect the kegs of brandy, bolts of silk and tobacco from the wine vaults under Mellin Hall.

'We must take these things back to the farm,' Hal instructed, leaping from the wagon and running round to help Wenna down. 'Pack everything into the back here, there's plenty of space.'

'What if the soldiers decide to search the farm too?' Hedra's brow was furrowed.

'I have a plan.' Hal grinned across at her. 'And if it works, as I'm sure it will, we need have no fear of them finding anything.'

'What plan?' Dewi asked.

'The fewer people who know about it, the more secure it will be, but I will need a few volunteers to accompany me and my brothers back to the farm.'

Five of the strongest men, plus Kit and Tomas, went back to Gribble Farm with the four Pentreath brothers, leaving Wenna chewing her lip and the two other women staring after them.

'You look pale, Dewi. Come inside and sit for a while,' Hedra said, sending a worried glance in the younger woman's direction. The three of them went indoors, and Hedra called for Jesemy to bring some warm milk. She sat Dewi in a chair by the fire.

'This has all been too much for you, but the contraband has all gone now. The danger has passed.'

'It's only been passed to Gribble Farm,' Dewi said quietly. 'I don't feel any happier about that.'

'But you heard what Hal said,' Wenna interrupted. 'He has a plan, and he sounded confident to me.'

Hedra nodded. 'Wenna's right. We must trust our men. They know what they are doing.'

Wenna was still savouring the phrase 'our men' when Jesemy appeared with a tray of tea and a glass of hot milk for Dewi.

'I told you, Miss Dewi, not to get yourself upset. It baint good for you to get upset, not in your condition.'

They all stared at her. 'Condition?' Dewi said. 'What condition, Jesemy? What are you talking about?'

'Well, the babe, of course. You 'ave to think of the babe now.' She looked round the three shocked faces and pressed her fingers to her lips. 'Oh, I'm sorry, Miss Dewi, I shouldn't 'ave spoke up. 'Taint my business to be speaking up.'

'I'm not with child, Jesemy. What made you say that?'

Jesemy gave her a long, knowing look. 'I know a woman with child when I see 'er. And you'd be a woman with child.'

Dewi put a hand gently on her abdomen. 'But I can't be.' She glanced across at Hedra. 'Can I?'

'Well, don't ask me,' Hedra laughed. 'But it strikes me that Jesemy is a wise old owl; and if she says you have a child on the way, then maybe we should just accept that and congratulate you.' She didn't wait for a response. She was out of her chair and throwing her arms around Dewi. Wenna bounced across the room and embraced both of them.

'Wait. Let's not be hasty,' Dewi

cautioned, but her eyes were shining. 'I have had no hint that I might be with child.'

'Reckon you must be very early on then, Miss Dewi,' Jesemy said, folding her arms across her large bosom and grinning from ear to ear.

'Oh dear,' Dewi said, sinking back in her chair. 'This is all so strange. But we must not make assumptions, at least not until I know for sure.' She looked at each woman in turn. 'And none of us must breathe a word about this outside this room. Promise me — especially not to Kit.'

'Of course not.' Hedra smiled. 'You must tell Kit yourself — when you know for certain, that is.'

* * *

'You be fortunate to still have your life, young man,' Annie said, looking down at the bruised figure in the cot bed. 'It was Hal Pentreath and our young Wenna that saved you.'

Enor lifted a shaky hand to his head. The movement caused a sharp pain to sear through him. He winced. 'What's happened to me?'

'You were found in the cave back there. Someone had near beaten the life out of you. Reckon they thought you were a goner.'

Enor screwed his eyes tight, trying to remember. Hazy images swam before him. It was dark . . . he was riding . . . there were others. They were shadowy figures he couldn't quite focus on. He squinted up at Annie. 'Who did this to me?'

'No point thinking on that now. You just concentrate on getting yourself fit again. I'll send word to your ma an' pa when you look a bit more respectable.'

Enor struggled to sit up, but the pain burned through him again. His whole body felt like all the wild stallions on the moor had stampeded over him. Brief flashes of memory swept before his eyes, but he couldn't make sense of any of them.

Annie had left the room and returned now with a bowl of thin porridge. 'It might not be easy to sup this up, but you should try. We need to build up your strength again.' She supported his head and spoon-fed him with the oaty mixture. Every swallow of the warm porridge was painful, but he knew he had to make the effort. When the bowl was empty he sank back onto the bed, exhausted.

Somewhere across the room he could hear a man's voice — Jory, probably. He couldn't focus his mind. All he wanted to do was sleep . . . sleep away the pain. He closed his eyes and prayed for the hazy darkness to wash over him again, but it didn't.

'How is your patient today?' Jory asked, giving his wife a quick peck on the cheek as he entered the room and glanced down at Enor.

'I believe he is a little better. He's managed a bowl of porridge, so that's no bad thing. I crushed a few chamomile leaves into it. He should sleep for a while.'

'I know Enor is family, Annie, but he has brought such shame on us. And what was he doing in that cave?'

Annie gave a defeated shrug but said nothing.

'Wenna says it was Trevanion's man who did this to him. Now what do you reckon he was doing with them?'

Annie sighed. 'I know. It doesn't look good, but we should give Enor a chance to explain before we condemn him.'

'He may die before that,' Jory said. 'And that may not be a bad thing.'

Annie flashed him a shocked look. She was speechless. How could her husband even think such a thing?

'You know in your heart that it's true, Annie. Enor came to Mellin Cove with the sole intention of making a false claim about his inheritance, and when young St Neot sent him packing he attempted to take his revenge out on all of us. Somehow he discovered what we used that cave for, and he betrayed us. Enor betrayed all of us.' He gave a weary sigh and shook his head. 'He used us, Annie, just as he used all of our friends down here. What kind of man does that? If the agent hadn't turned up earlier than expected and taken the goods away, that cave would have been packed with brandy and all the rest. The revenue officers would have arrested every man and woman in the cove — including us. We would all have been thrown into Bodmin Jail, maybe even hanged. Are you surprised I have no concern whether Enor Vingoe lives or dies?'

Annie stared bleakly out of the tiny window and out to the choppy water of the harbour. She shook her head. 'Not everyone feels as you do, Jory. Lots of our friends have knocked at the door and enquired after him. Even the St Neots called in.' She pointed. 'They left that basket of eggs, and Jesemy sent some fresh bread and biscuits for him.'

'That's because our friends are kind, Annie,' he said, putting his arms around his wife's shoulders as they left the room. 'Not because Enor deserves it.'

After they'd gone, the figure on the cot bed remained motionless, absorbing the silence around him. A shudder swept through his battered body and he blinked, feeling the wetness on his cheeks. Enor Vingoe was crying!

He lay in his narrow bed that night listening to the buzz of voices that drifted up from the kiddley. He knew that Annie and Jory would be in there serving ale to thirsty customers and keeping an eye on the more rowdy ones. He was alone in the cottage. Carefully he eased himself up from the bed, every movement causing him flashes of intense pain. He winced as he hauled himself upright. His first few steps were unsteady, so he took his time, but eventually he felt confident enough to reach the cottage door and step out onto the harbourside.

The salty air hit him in a blast, and he sucked it into his lungs as he steadied himself on the doorjamb. If he managed to reach the far side of the harbour and then walk back, he would be well on the way to recovery. And Enor was determined to recover his strength as quickly as possible now. He had a job to do, and it would take every ounce of his strength if he were to succeed.

Annie and Jory took no care about what they discussed in front of him. They assumed him to be sleeping most of the day, but Enor had heard it all. When Wenna had come to call, he heard her tell Annie how Sir Bartholomew had betrayed the village. It was not news to him that Trevanion was no friend of Mellin Cove. Had he not depended on that very thing when he offered to lead him and his man to the cave where the smuggled goods were stored? Shame crept over Enor when he remembered what he had done. Well, he had to make amends now. Many bridges had to be built, but first he must settle his differences with Sir Bartholomew Trevanion.

It was easy to sneak out of the

cottage unseen while Annie and Jory were busy in the kiddley. Finding his way across the moor to Lanyon Manor in the dark was a lot more difficult than the first time he'd done it. Annie had wound tight bandages around his chest to ease the pain of what were certainly cracked ribs. The discomfort slowed his progress, and he'd stumbled more than once, almost tipping himself into a gorse bush. The pain was a harsh reminder of why his plan *had* to succeed.

Lights blazed from all the ground floor windows of the hall, but Enor was interested in the servants' quarters. He stole around the back of the building, hesitating when he spotted the stairs down to a basement door.

Gripping the metal bannister for support, he moved silently down. The door opened easily and he slipped inside. He was in a dimly lit corridor; the flickering candles in sconces on the walls were casting moving shadows. Somewhere up ahead he could hear the rattle of dishes, and guessed it came from the kitchen, where maids would be washing the crockery from Sir Bartholomew's evening meal. He stepped closer, straining his ears to hear the voices.

'Tom Swayne be no better than my Colin, yet he treats him like a bad smell.'

'He's a dangerous one, that one. You should stay well clear, Maisie.'

'Dangerous?' the first voice said. 'You mean the man is a thug?'

'I've heard tell he makes people disappear and thinks nothing of it. You should stay clear, I tell you.'

'Happen the Master needs to know what kind of man he employs.'

'Don't you be the one to tell him, Maisie, or you could be one of them that disappears.'

Enor heard Maisie give a loud sniff. 'I know other things Tom Swayne would not want making public.'

'Is this another one of your stories, Maisie Bilton? You don't want to be tangling with that man, or I'll be needing to find another kitchen maid; for sure as eggs is eggs, you will be dead and gone.'

'You're talking nonsense, Susan. If I go to the Master with what I know, lord high and mighty Tom will be out of Lanyon Manor quicker than he can blow his nose.'

Susan sighed. 'So what is this great secret you know?'

'Shush. Keep your voice down. I don't want everyone to hear what I know.'

There was a pause, and Enor wondered if the women had left the kitchen. He moved his weight from one foot to the other and put his hands on his sides to ease his aching ribs.

'Where do you think he is at this very moment?' Maisie's voice was conspiratorial. 'Out in the stables, that's where. I saw him just now when I crossed the yard.'

'I don't see why that is such a secret,' Susan said.

‘It’s who he is with, silly. It’s who he’s got in there with him.’ She gave a course laugh. ‘And they weren’t grooming the horses.’

Enor hadn’t been looking for the stables when he’d crept round the house, but now he thought back to the buildings around the rear yard. He could picture which one was the stables.

He left the house as silently as he had entered it and made his way back up the steps. The yard was in darkness, but he could make out the stables without any trouble. He held his sides as he skirted the yard, staying close to the buildings. When he reached the wide entrance to the stables he paused, listening. A horse whinnied from somewhere inside — and then he heard a woman giggle. Enor held his breath.

‘Keep your voice down, Carolyn. Do you want the Master to find us?’

Enor froze. It was him! He would have recognized the man’s voice anywhere. It was the last voice he’d heard that night in the cave before the pain tore through his body and his world plunged into blackness.

He could feel fury rising in him. His intention had been to surprise the man, sneak up behind him with a hammer and give him the beating he had been subjected to. But now a better plan was coming together. If this was the Carolyn he thought it was, then all he had to do was to go to Trevanion. The pair were not only carrying on, but they were doing it under Sir Bartholomew's own roof.

The last time he'd been to Lanyon Manor, he had been shown into a study. Could he find his way there by himself? Yes, why not? He didn't see the young maid, Maisie, carry a brandy decanter into that very room, but he watched from outside the window as Sir Bartholomew unfolded a note he'd found on his desk and began to read it. Enor continued to gaze with curiosity at the scene before him.

Suddenly he saw the jowly face turn

purple and Sir Bartholomew's eyes bulge. The man's roar could be heard all the way across the moors. 'Carolyn!' he yelled, leaping to his feet and hurrying from the room. 'Carolyn!'

The man appeared to be incandescent with rage. He strode across the yard, heading for the stables. '*Carolyn!*' He stormed into the stables.

Enor had followed with growing amusement, keeping to the shadows. It sounded like a great civil war had broken out inside.

Lady Carolyn was the first to emerge, clutching her skirts as she desperately tried to keep her unstrung bodice together. She fled across the yard in a flurry of flapping silk. Enor could hear the roar of Sir Bartholomew's voice from inside the stables. 'I want you out of my house *now* — right this minute!' he roared.

'This is not what it seems, sir. Please allow me to explain.' Tom Swayne's voice sounded desperate.

'Do not insult my intelligence, man.

You have disgraced my daughter. I should have you horsewhipped for this.'

The idea obviously took hold in Sir Bartholomew's mind, for the words were hardly out when Tom Swayne sprinted out of the stables, his breeches under his arm. Sir Bartholomew was on his heels, cracking a horsewhip at him. Tom leapt across the cobbled yard, picking up his bare feet with a yell as he stepped on horse droppings.

Enor grinned, holding his sides as the rumble of laughter bubbled up inside him. The man who had attacked him so viciously was being well and truly dealt with, and he hadn't needed to lift a finger. Lady Carolyn had no doubt taken flight to her bedchamber and wouldn't venture out again that night. Tom Swayne had been banished from Lanyon Manor in disgrace. But Enor was still curious about Trevanion. He followed the man back to his study, and watched again from the window.

Sir Bartholomew wasn't alone. The window was open, but only by an inch or so. It was enough for Enor to hear at least part of the conversation taking place inside. He got closer to the gap.

'I don't understand,' Trevanion's voice boomed. 'I told you they hide the goods in the cave. Why are you not instructing the soldiers to search there?'

The stranger's voice was calmer. 'These people are clever, which is why we must be careful. They will know their secret hiding place is a secret no longer and they will act accordingly.'

'What do you mean?'

'Which would you consider to be the next most unlikely place in Mellin Cove to hide treasure?'

Sir Bartholomew frowned. 'The Hall,' he said. 'I've already told you those devils will hide their contraband at Mellin Hall.'

'Exactly.'

'So you will search Mellin Hall?'

'Of course we will. But even if we find what we are looking for, it will not implicate the people, only the St Neots.'

'You will have to explain that to me,' Trevanion said. 'The people are undoubtedly involved in these illegal activities. They should be punished.'

'And indeed they will be,' the stranger said. 'The soldiers will be instructed to search the cottages down by the harbour. They may feel the need to torch a few of them.'

Enor felt his blood running cold. He was torn between rushing back to the cove to warn Annie, Jory and the others about what he'd just heard, and staying put to hear what else might be said. He decided he needed to hear the full story. There was no point taking back half a tale.

'What about the fishing boats?' Trevanion was asking.

'The boats are what these people use to bring in the contraband,' the visitor said. Enor saw the man's shoulders lift in a shrug. 'We cannot allow that to continue.'

'What do you mean?'

'I mean they must be destroyed, and

they will be. Tomorrow evening after dark, the Mellin Cove fishing fleet will be no more!'

# 19

Enor Vingoe was back in the cot bed in the Rosens' front room. He lay staring at the ceiling, hearing every creak and twinge of the old cottage as it settled in for the night. If he glanced at the small window to his right, he could see the stars. Surely dawn could not be far off now. The thought caused his heart to beat faster. He still was uncertain whether waiting for morning before taking any action had been the right decision, but what could anyone have done sooner? There was always the possibility that no one would trust him. He had given them enough reason to be wary of him; he knew that.

Enor's head was so full of angst that he'd hardly noticed the first streaks of light in the sky. Somewhere in the cottage someone was stirring. Annie, he thought. She always rose early. She would be the first to hear what he had discovered. She would know what to do. But it was Jory he found in the kitchen, cursing under his breath at the fire's reluctance to ignite.

'So you've decided to rise from your comfortable bed and join the rest of the world at last,' he said sharply.

Enor ignored the jibe. He would have to get used to comments like this. 'I was looking for Annie,' he said.

Jory nodded to the door to where she stood fiddling with unruly strands of hair that refused to be secured with her pins. 'Enor!' Her smile was genuine. 'You're feeling better?'

'I need to speak to you both,' he said. 'I've discovered something.'

Annie and Jory listened, shaking their heads in disbelief as he repeated the conversation he'd heard while crouching outside the window of Sir Bartholomew Trevanion's study.

Jory gave him a suspicious look. 'What were you doing there?'

'I went to confront Trevanion and his

man, Swayne. They were the ones who beat me and left me for dead in the cave, but that is not important now. What I've just told you is serious. We have to warn Kit St Neot and the others. We have to stop this happening.'

'He's telling the truth, Jory. Just look at him.'

'I've done some terrible things, I know that,' Enor said desperately. 'And I do not expect anyone in Mellin Cove to forgive me. But you must believe I am telling the truth now. No one deserves to have their home burned to the ground, or their fishing boat destroyed. You have to trust me, Jory.'

'I don't trust you, Enor. But I will go with you to Mellin Hall.'

Enor's thank-you came out in a relieved sigh.

* * *

'Jem needs to hear this, and Hal, too,' Kit said when he had heard Enor's story. He called for Tomas. It was a further twenty minutes before the brothers arrived, summoned by an anxious Tomas. The six men crowded into Kit's study and fell silent while Enor retold his story.

When he had finished, Kit frowned, turning to Jory. 'What do you make of this?' He slid a less than trusting glance to Enor. 'Can we believe this tale?'

'Of course you must believe me,' Enor burst out. 'Why would I make up a thing like this? You may despise me for what I have done, but I'm trying to help you now.'

Jory gave a reluctant nod. 'Annie believes him. I don't see how we can afford to ignore his story.'

'It is not the story Carolyn told you, Kit,' Jem said, 'but of course things could have moved on since then.'

'The man Trevanion was speaking with did mention something about his previous visit to Lanyon Manor,' Enor said. 'I got the impression that what they were discussing was a newer plan.'

Hal stepped into the middle of the

room. 'Even if the soldiers search the cottages, they won't find anything. The action we took yesterday will ensure that.'

'They could still burn the cottages,' Jem said grimly.

'The first thing you must do, Jem, is to get the boats away,' Kit said.

'You're right. I'll alert all the crews. We can anchor the luggers around the headland. They will be safe there.'

'We still need a plan,' Hal said.

'What about a fire?' Tomas cut in. 'We could set blazes up on the cliff top — a line of fire that would prevent the soldiers from reaching the cove.'

'But how do we stop the whole moor from going up? The bracken is tinder-dry out there,' Kit said.

'What about the pond?' Hal offered. 'If we saturated the area around the fires with pond water, then it would give us some control over the flames spreading.'

'It's still risky,' Kit said.

'Not as risky as allowing the soldiers

to torch the cottages,' Jem said. 'I don't see what choice we have.'

'It doesn't stop the soldiers coming back, though,' Hal said. 'If the authorities are convinced that smuggling activities are taking place in the cove, they will return.'

'I have an idea about that,' Enor said quietly.

* * *

Luncheon at Boscawen House was not a pleasurable event at the best of times, but when Wenna's father was absent it was barely courteous. Her grandmother sat with her usual poker-stiff back, picking at her food with an expression of distaste, while her stepmother cleared her plate with a speed that bordered on gluttony. Neither of them spoke, or even acknowledged that Wenna was there. She waited until the main course plates had been cleared before saying, 'I will be staying at Mellin Cove tonight with Annie and Jory.'

Lady Catherine glared at her. 'Are you planning to move into that hovel on a permanent basis?'

Wenna sighed. 'It is not a hovel, Grandmother. You know perfectly well that Annie would never keep a house like that. They are my friends. I enjoy visiting them.'

Her grandmother gave a disapproving tut. 'I notice it is only when your father is away on his parliamentary business that you do this.'

Wenna's stepmother waved a hand, dismissing the conversation. 'Let her go, Catherine. Why should we care? Wenna is doing what she always does — behaving like a gipsy girl.'

A curt rebuke was on the tip of Wenna's tongue. Who were these women to criticize her when they were prepared to cheat and steal and hurt people for their own greedy ends? Lady Catherine Quintrell might be her grandmother, but Wenna had no respect for the woman, not anymore. As for her stepmother, well she could never understand why her father had married her.

She glanced from one to the other. They probably believed, wrongly, that they were safe from any further action she might take over their piracy activities. In truth, she hadn't yet decided how to deal with that. She'd confided in her friends at the cove of course, but the issue had been overtaken by so many other serious events.

It was mid-afternoon when Wenna crossed the moors to Mellin Cove and stopped in her tracks. In the distance she could see much activity. It appeared as though the entire population of the cove was up here cutting bracken. She had never seen anything like it. What was going on? She stood staring for a moment as more and more of the busy figures became familiar. Hal! Jem was there too, and their younger brothers. And then Kit and his man Tomas came into view, staggering under the weight of buckets.

Wenna hurried on, frowning, until she came within shouting distance of Hal. Putting up a hand to shield her eyes from the sun, she called out to him. He waved when he saw her, beckoning her forward.

'What's happening?' she said, her eyes sweeping over the buzz of people who seemed to be swarming everywhere.

'The soldiers are coming tonight,' he said. 'We have to stop them getting down to the cove and burning the cottages.'

Wenna stared at him. 'They're going to burn the village? But why?'

'It's a long story. We can talk when we have finished here.'

Wenna pushed up her sleeves. 'Tell me what to do. I can help.'

The way Hal tilted his head and looked at her made her heart quicken. And then he smiled, pointing across to where a group of women were hacking through the bracken. 'They could probably do with an extra pair of hands.'

It was another two hours before they

had finished. Wenna stretched up, easing the stiffness from her back. 'I've told my family I'm staying with Annie and Jory tonight and I haven't even asked them,' she told Hal when he came to join her.

'I'll walk down to the cove with you,' he said.

When they reached the cottage, to Wenna's surprise, Hal came in behind her. Annie's eyes lit up when she saw Wenna.

'Would it be too much of an imposition if I asked to stay the night?' she asked.

To her dismay, Annie shook her head. 'That's not a good idea, Wenna. Mellin Cove could be a very dangerous place tonight. Your father would never forgive me if anything happened to you.'

'Annie's right, but I wanted you to hear it from her,' Hal said quietly. 'You should go home tonight and come back in the morning when this is all over.'

'What — turn my back on my friends when they could be in danger? I would never do that.' Wenna was furious. 'I'll sleep up on the moors if I have to, but I am not going home.'

Hal sighed and gave her a look that said, *Why are you so stubborn?* 'You won't have to sleep on the moors. You can come back to the farm with me. You will have to bed down with my sister Queenie, mind, but I'm sure Ma will make you welcome.'

Wenna looked at him through lowered lashes. 'I promise not to be any trouble,' she said meekly.

Hal shook his head. 'There are conditions.'

She blinked.

'You do not, under any circumstances, leave the farmhouse after dark tonight. Is that understood?'

Wenna nodded.

* * *

The evening meal at Gribble Farm was eaten to an accompaniment of excited family babble. It was a very different experience to what Wenna was used to when dining at Boscawen House. She was in no doubt about which she preferred.

No one knew how successful the efforts of the people that afternoon would be in keeping the soldiers out of the cove, but there was a feeling of confidence in the air.

'There's something else going on, isn't there?' Wenna whispered to Hal after she had helped Sally and Queenie clear the supper table and wash the plates. She followed him out to the yard. 'There's something you haven't told me.' She watched him gaze along the cliff path and saw the men coming towards them.

He stepped forward, raising his arm in greeting as Kit, Tomas, Jem, and Enor Vingoe walked into the yard.

'Luk has dug the goods up again. They are over here. We'll need the wagon,' Hal said.

'What's going on?' Wenna hissed. 'What goods have been dug up?'

'The less you know, the better,' Hal said. 'Please go back indoors now and help Ma.'

'Do as Hal says, Wenna . . . for all our sakes,' Enor said.

She felt like stamping her foot and telling them not to treat her like a child, but a glance around the serious faces told her not to. Without another word, she turned and walked slowly back to the farmhouse.

Sally Pentreath was alone in the kitchen when she went in. 'Do you know what's happening out there?' Wenna asked.

'Best we don't talk about it,' Sally said. 'The fewer people who know about this, the better.'

'It's to do with the soldiers, isn't it?'

Sally pressed her lips together and said nothing.

* * *

None of the five men spoke as the wagon rumbled over the rough moorland track to Lanyon Manor. They stopped as they approached the place, tying rags around the horse's hooves and the wheels of the wagon to muffle the sound. Enor pointed to where the stables were as they followed him into the yard.

Quietly they unpacked the wagon, each man hardly daring to breathe as he carried his load across the cobbles. Once a light flickered in one of the downstairs windows, but Enor whispered it would be a candle held by a passing servant, who wouldn't be able to see out into the dark courtyard.

It took six heart-stopping trips from the wagon to the stables to complete their task. Once it was done, Hal led his horse silently away. They waited until they were well across the moors before punching the air in triumph.

'Did we really do that?' Tomas's eyes in the darkness were wide with shocked laughter.

Kit patted him on the back. 'We really did. Now we need to put the second part of the plan into action.'

They hid amongst the gorse and bracken of the moor for what seemed like hours before they heard the tramp of the soldiers' boots.

'Something's not right,' Hal said. 'Why are they making no attempt to conceal themselves? It's as though they want us to hear them.'

Other men from the cove were breaking cover. He could hear stirrings all across the area where they had earlier cut the bracken and stacked it ready for lighting.

Kit and Jem crawled up to him. Kit's whisper was urgent. 'I think they are going in the other direction. They're not making for the cove.'

Enor rolled across the rough ground to join them. 'They're heading for Lanyon Manor,' he said.

'They couldn't have found the contraband, not yet,' Hal said.

Enor was thinking. There was one person who now had as much hatred for Sir Bartholomew Trevanion as he did: his attacker, Tom Swayne. What if

Swayne had returned to the stables in search of some item of property he'd left there? What if he discovered the contraband? But he wouldn't care if it had been planted on Trevanion. He would just want the man to suffer.

A slow smile began to spread across Enor Vingoe's face. 'I think our plan has worked, gentlemen.'

# 20

It was the following morning before the news of Sir Bartholomew Trevanion's arrest reached Mellin Cove. Enor was the first to hear, which was probably because he had sneaked back to Lanyon Manor in the early hours to do some more eavesdropping at open windows.

'And we didn't have to torch the moor,' Annie said, her eyes shining.

'Not only that,' Enor said, 'but I doubt if the authorities will have any suspicions about Mellin Cove now. From what I heard this morning, they believe Sir Bartholomew was trying to steer them in that direction to cover up his own illegal activities.'

'Even if he was not actually doing anything illegal?' Annie giggled.

'Oh, believe me, that man would definitely have been up to something,' Jory said. 'Perhaps not this particular something, but justice has a way of asserting itself. We need feel no remorse in that direction.'

'And what about you now?' Annie asked Enor. 'Will you stay on in the cove?'

Enor looked out across the harbour and sighed. 'I think not. I have a hankering to be home.'

Jory put a hand on his shoulder. 'Reckon I misjudged you, young Enor, and for that I am sorry.'

But Enor shook his head. 'You didn't misjudge me, sir. I deserved all your harsh words. Happen it just took me a bit longer than most to grow up.'

* * *

Dewi slipped out of bed before Kit was awake. She stood watching him for a moment before hugging herself and going to the window. The world looked gloriously rosy. Fingers of crimson, purple and gold streaked across the sky, turning the ocean to fire. Down in the cove she could see the tops of the fishing boats' masts bobbing. They would not go to sea this morning. This was to be a day of celebration in Mellin Cove. They had fought the dragon — and they had won.

She felt a shiver of excitement as her hands caressed her abdomen — her abdomen that was fertile with a child. She was certain of that now.

Behind her Kit stirred and stretched. 'Why have you risen so early?' he said sleepily.

She half-turned, aware that he was getting up and coming to her. She felt his arms go around her, holding her close. 'I have something to tell you, Kit,' she said softly.

He rested his chin on her shoulder, gazing out to sea. 'I don't think I could ever be happier than I am at this very moment,' he said.

She turned to look into his eyes. 'I believe you may be,' she said, as he took her face in his hands and kissed her.

* * *

'Will you come home with me, Hal? There is something you need to see,' Wenna said, coming out to the yard and wiping her hands on the apron that Sally had tied around her waist as she'd washed the breakfast dishes. No one at Gribble Farm had slept much the previous night. There had been too much celebrating to do.

Hal stared at her. 'To Boscawen House? I'm not sure that would be a good idea.'

'Why not? You won't have to meet my family or anything like that.' She smiled. 'Well, maybe just my grandmother. But believe me, after what she has done, she will not be putting on any airs and graces.'

'And what do you think the servants will say when we pull up in front of your grand house in my old farm wagon?'

She gave him a chiding look. 'You are such a snob, Hal. The servants are my friends. Why would you be concerned what they think? I doubt very much if my father will be home. He seems to spend all his time in London now. So what do you say? Will you come with me?'

He tilted his head and grinned at her. 'You leave me no choice! I'll dust down the wagon.'

It was almost an hour before they trundled up the drive to Boscawen House. Hal heaved a sigh of relief to see there was no reception committee. Wenna leapt down from the wagon before he was able to help her. 'The things I want to show you are in my grandmother's room,' she said. 'She will be in the morning room doing whatever it is she does in there at this time of day. I have a key.'

Hal felt uncomfortable as he followed Wenna inside the grand house, up the flight of marble stairs, and along the landing.

'This is my bedchamber,' Wenna said. 'You can wait at the door here while I fetch the key.'

Hal studied the portraits lining the walls and wondered if they were Wenna's ancestors. He pictured the rooms at Gribble Farm, homely in their way, but nothing like the elegance that now surrounded him. He began to fidget, wishing he had never come. He felt like a fish out of water in this elegant house. As soon as one of Wenna's family discovered his presence, he would surely be thrown out.

'I have it,' Wenna said, emerging from her chamber waving a small silver key. 'It's just this way.'

Hal followed, glancing uneasily around him. Wenna led him into an elegant lavender-smelling bedchamber dominated by a large oak four-poster bed that was hung with swathes of lilac taffeta and trimmed with frills of white lace. A large dressing table overflowed with bottles and jars of every size.

'As you can see, my grandmother likes her colognes,' Wenna said, inserting the key into the lock. The door to the anteroom swung open. 'This is what I wanted you to see,' she said, stepping inside.

Hal gasped. The walls were piled high with boxes and velvet purses of all colours and sizes. 'Is this what I think it is?' He swallowed.

'My grandmother's booty,' Wenna said. 'I think we should take it all back to Mellin Hall, whence we can distribute it. I'm not happy that it is still here.'

Hall frowned. He was trying to work out how such treasures could be safely transported. One thing was clear — the farm wagon would certainly not do. Perhaps Kit would offer his coach.

Wenna smiled at him. 'You're wondering how we can get all of this to Mellin Hall.' He nodded. 'Easy.' She laughed. 'We have several family coaches, but I will need your help to put the boxes and things into plain sacks. We shouldn't make it obvious what the contents are.'

'I would agree with that,' Hal said.

'When do you plan to do all this?'

'We must first ask Kit and Dewi if they will allow us to bring these treasures to Mellin Hall.'

'Would you like me to ask the St Neots when I get back to the cove? If they agree, then we could return in the morning to do what is necessary.'

The room was small and they were standing very close to each other. Wenna longed for him to reach out for her, to take her in his arms, but she knew he wouldn't. Bringing him to Boscawen had been a mistake; she had just destroyed whatever relationship they had. But he needed to see the home where she had been brought up. The time for deception had passed. He needed to see the lifestyle her family enjoyed, even if she knew he would not appreciate it. It would take time — years perhaps — before she made Hal realize that no matter how different their worlds were, they were meant for each other.

She made to leave, but he put a hand

on her back and turned her slowly to face him. Wenna's heart pounded so wildly it would surely burst right out of her. They were inches apart, suspended in time, neither of them daring to move.

She blinked. Hal's hands were exploring her face with such gentleness. Her lips trembled under his touch. She closed her eyes and his mouth came down on hers. For long, glorious moments they clung together, neither of them wanting the kiss to end.

When it did, Hal drew away sharply, his head in his hands. 'Forgive me, Wenna. I had no right to do that. I . . . '

But she had stopped him with another kiss. 'I love you, Hal Pentreath,' she murmured. 'I love you so much.'

Hal stroked her hair. 'I cannot compete with the life you have here, Wenna. I'm only a poor farmer. I can offer you nothing.'

She pulled back, staring at him. 'If you think I care anything for this life, then you are wrong.'

'But you will come to care. Boscawen

is your inheritance. All I can offer is a rather meagre existence on a moorland farm. It would be demeaning for you to settle for that.'

They had moved slowly from the room where Lady Catherine stored her treasures and were now passing the portraits of Wenna's ancestors.

'I hadn't noticed Hedra *demeaning* herself to marry your brother, Jem,' she said. 'She doesn't seem to mind that her home is now a humble cottage and not a great manor house. I have never known a more devoted couple.'

'That's different,' Hal said.

But Wenna could see he was wavering. She smiled. She might still have some persuading to do. She stretched up to kiss him again, abandoning herself to the delicious sensation of Hal's mouth on hers.

Wenna knew there was no hurry. She could wait. She sighed. The persuasion was going to be sweet . . .

*Other titles in the Linford Romance Library:*

## SUMMER LOVE

### Jill Barry

1966: When Liz Lane arrives at Rainbows Holiday Camp in Devon to work as secretary to the entertainments manager, she is thrown into a world of sand, sun and fun, despite the long hours. Her boss suspects his new secretary will be a hit with the holidaymakers, and before long Liz is wearing a Rainbows uniform. But she ends up at loggerheads with Rob, the chief host, despite their mutual attraction to each other. Will love find a way?

## FALLING FOR DR. RIGHT

**Jo Bartlett**

In the wake of her mother's death and a broken engagement, Dr. Evie Daniels decides to travel the world, doing everything her mum never had the chance to. Leaving her London job, she accepts a temporary locum position in the remote Scottish town of Balloch Pass, where she finds herself enjoying the work and community — and her handsome colleague Dr. Alasdair James. The feeling is mutual — but Alasdair is bound to Balloch Pass, whilst Evie is committed to spreading her wings . . .